DREAM STATE

A NOVEL

BY MARTIN OTT

CASTLE BRIDGE MEDIA
DENVER, COLORADO, USA

CASTLE BRIDGE MEDIA
Denver, Colorado

Cover photo by Jordan Steranka/Unsplash

DREAM STATE
© 2022 Martin Ott
All rights reserved.

ISBN: 979-8-9859702-0-3

CHAPTER 1

Heidi Radar

SOME SCIENTISTS ARGUED THAT OCTOPI and squids were more intelligent, but Heidi couldn't imagine how that could be true. The two bottle-nosed dolphins had been trained by the previous staff to clear underwater mines. To identify enemy swimmers. Her current boyfriend Petty Officer Rick Coslow had hinted that they could be strapped with explosives to take down enemy vessels. Heidi assumed he was joking but she was out of her element in her tumultuous relationship with him and with her duties at the advanced SEAL Demolition Training Center on one of the remote islands off the coast of Belize that Belizeans call "caves." She'd taken over caring for the animals on an interim basis after the previous trainer went native in Belize City. Rick had discovered she had a degree in zoology (OK so she'd never actually graduated after failing Calculus three times) one day on the beach at Copeland Resort, the caye's only tourist accommodation, after she set up her towel next to his after a swim.

How in the hell had she ended up here of all places?

She remembered a series of strip bars she worked at after failing out of UCLA, taking the stage name *Tarzana*, the valley town she grew up in. Her mother Mona was an artist who hadn't needed to work, falling in with a string of men to pay her bills, starting with Heidi's Brazilian father. Why should Heidi be any different? A man had paid for her to come to the resort, a music producer who'd threatened to withhold her ticket home unless she had sex with him. Problem solved when she hooked up with Rick and took him up on his offer to stay with him. Her legal status was in flux with her visa in the process of being updated by Commander Owen Frank, a brown-haired man with good posture and flecks of gray over his ears, who reminded her of her own father. Her dad Marcos Radar was German-Brazilian and lived in Sao Paulo. She was like any other valley white girl except for her haphazard Portuguese honed from summers visiting her father.

Dad was a businessman who'd encouraged her interest in animals and used his influence to get her positions at zoological parks, and later as an assistant for field work in the rain forest. She'd stopped talking to him and her mother after she dropped out of college. Without the diploma she was flotsam. She was depressed. She was bedlam in human form. Her exotic dancing gig to pay for college turned into a career. The drugs she took to make the enterprise easier became an addiction. She'd lost herself in E and meth, in pot to even herself out, in the attention of men for self-worth. She'd been a hot mess in a city of hot messes.

Oddly enough, it was a week at Copeland Caye that had given her a chance to sober up off the harder drugs, to think clearly for the first time in years. She was close to calling her parents. She was close to imagining a future beyond dawn after a night of all-night partying when the Special Warfare Combat Craft (SWCC) revved toward the naval dock with their recent batch of trainees, a squad of SEALs receiving specialty training in munitions. There were a lot of things to get used to here: the acronyms, the testosterone, and the munitions that could send them all to the next world, whatever that was. She did not believe in God, although she sometimes prayed, another habit inherited from her mother Mona. Catholic guilt without the trappings.

Rick leapt off the boat and tied it to the dock area, where a second boat was moored. The engine cut off and the other men began gathering their gear. She could see the outline of the dolphins bobbing behind the vehicles. The docks, unlike the one at Copeland Resort, had corrugated tin roofs that stretched above the equipment to protect it from the elements. Mostly. Flo and Jet, dolphin sisters, splashed their way toward Heidi. She jumped into the water and led them into a small lagoon that funneled to the side of the docks and was surrounded by mesh fencing that stretched to the ocean bottom.

The dolphins had taught her their routine for feeding by trial and error. They preferred to be hand-fed, even though she could easily have dumped the fish she procured from D-town, the only village on the island, into their pen. Perhaps the former trainer had done it this way to bond the mammals to them. She was the one, though, who was putty around the two of them even as she felt guilty. They belonged out in the ocean. They, unlike her, had not volunteered to be here.

The trainees hustled from the boat to store their equipment in lockers and hurried to get changed. It was Friday and the squad was taking the ferry (which ran twice a week) to Vista Del Mar, a village just north of Belize City. Their island was more remote than most of the cayes, further to the north and nearly fifteen miles from the capital. Rick padded over to her with his wetsuit peeled down to reveal his muscular chest. His appearance was like that of a prehistoric caveman, Fred Flintstone in the flesh, with broad shoulders, square feet, wide jaw and forehead, two hundred and twenty pounds of muscle, easily twice her weight. He was a simple man with a deep voice and an endearing/occasionally annoying habit of trilling his voice like a boy when he asked a question.

"Hey, babe, what are you up to?" he asked in his signature singsong lilt.

"Making sure our dolphin friends are fed and didn't get injured. What did you guys do out there today?"

"Mostly, we just splashed around in the ocean trying not to get hurt."

"It's hard to teach guys how to blow shit up without actually blowing shit up," Heidi said.

"That's right. Mock training for wars we hope never happen."

"Amen," Heidi said, brushing her hair into her eyes instead of out of them, subconsciously hiding the circles, the insomnia and even worse problems.

"OK, spill? Where did you sleepwalk to this time?"

Rick was a goon, at times, but seemed to know whenever she was upset. She'd been sleepwalking in the fort, something she hadn't done since she was a child and had gotten up to unlock every door before going back to sleep.

"The basement, the supply cabinet. I was sorting. Again." That morning she'd found herself labeling the food with a sharpie, ink on masking tape. She'd sleep-walked down the stairs from the kitchen into the basement supply room and sometime storm shelter. She had grown accustomed to wearing clothes so that when Rick snuck out at dawn to lead his men on exercises, she wouldn't be found wandering the hallways sleepwalking in her skivvies.

"Maybe you should talk to someone about it," he suggested.

"I do. I talk to you."

He laughed and brushed her hair out of her eyes, grinning. "OK, gorgeous, I've got to boogie. I'd better babysit these goons to make sure everything gets put back before they storm off for the weekend."

"OK, gorgeous," she said.

"Catch you later at Cava then." And with that he was gone, never quite sure what to do when she parroted his sexist terms of endearment back to him. She had no doubt they would get drunk again on cheap rum in the island's only bar, between the base and the resort, where they were regulars.

After feeding the dolphins she took the time to do a visual inspection. She ran her fingers along the dorsal fins, each of the dolphins vying for her attention. She enjoyed her time with her frolicsome girls, the exercise and companionship, more likely to place her trust in any form of critter that wasn't human. Rick was one of the rare examples, and she reminded him of a dog, a simple creature. Trustworthy to a fault. Rigid in his beliefs in the American way and herself, both flawed totems. He would be mortified if he knew about her past.

She lost herself in her assignment. The dolphins had no abrasions from the training exercise. Their appetites were good. She tried to pace them in their laps around the pen, trying to burn away all vestiges of herself. She remembered her time on the stage and on the pole, her lust to turn men into savages, to earn their money and trust. She'd needed her next fix and lost herself and many friends along the way.

"Commander Frank wants to see you," a voice bounced across the water like a stone just before it sank.

Heidi shielded her eyes from the setting sun and climbed out of the water, drinking in her visitor in uniform.

"I'm Clint Jenkins," he said, leaning against the industrial fridge where they kept the fish.

"Heidi Radar," she said, "And you're one of the trainees?"

"Guilty as charged," he said.

She felt self-conscious in her two-piece suit as she reached into her locker and dried herself off. There was something about the SEAL that made her queasy. She was used to men looking at her with lust, but this guy regarded her like a half-eaten sandwich, trying to figure out if it was worth it to take a bite. Clint was tall and gangly, with red hair and freckles tattooing his sunburnt skin. His smile was a terrible thing to behold, all guile.

"Thank you," she said.

"You're welcome."

"That was also meant as a hint to leave while I get dressed."

"Suit yourself," he said. "That's a pun. Think about it."

Heidi was not shy, never had been, and her time as an exotic dancer and spending most of her life in beach attire the past few weeks made her comfortable with her skin on display. This time, though, she kept her wet swimsuit on as she pulled on a pair of jean shorts and a red flannel shirt.

She turned around but Clint was gone. *Idiotic pun for an idiotic punk*, she thought. Rick had told her how Clint thought of himself as the squad jester. He'd gotten caught breaking curfew and wouldn't be accompanying the rest of his training team on leave. He would be assisting Landry, their civilian clerk, with any number of odd jobs from carpentry to plumbing to cooking.

She heard the whoops from the crew racing out of the compound and hauling ass over the one mile of dirt road to the resort dock to board the ferry. The last one in the race would have to pay for the booze and lord knew what else in Belize City, using a rundown motel in Vista Del Mar as a launch pad for debauchery. The naval base was little more than a retrofitted mansion. In fact, it had belonged to a former drug smuggler before the Belize government gave it to the US Army, among other property, as a good-will gesture to keep the cash flowing to fight the drug war. The building was constructed like a fortress, with ten-foot-high stone walls and iron doors that made it, and the massive basement, the safest structure on the island during the tropical storms. Her room was the only one below ground, to separate her from the trainees.

Commander Frank's office was in a tower, the only vantage point in the compound from which the resort was visible. To reach the office you had to climb a broad staircase that fanned out and up from the front door that led to a courtyard and wrought-iron gate, the only entrance to the walled estate. Heidi was aware of the unusual silence in the building and made an effort not to make noise. She wasn't sure why. She didn't want to stir up anything out of the shadows.

She reached the waiting area outside the Commander's office. Normally, Landry, the other civilian employee on the base, would be waiting to greet her. Landry was an Englishman, who'd grown up in various Caribbean islands, and seemed little more than a domesticated servant: part assistant, cook, driver, whatever the Commander or the compound needed. Heidi wasn't even sure if Landry was his first or last name. He was always formally dressed, even in the heat, and had a natural reserve to him. Some sadness in his past. Or else, like herself, he had something to hide. She tapped on the office door and a voice called out "Come in."

She slid into the room and Commander Frank motioned for her to sit in a chair beside him. The office had a strange vibe, the mishmash of decorations from a military man overlaid on top of the garish, drug-dealer chic of its former occupant. The whole facility was a party house masquerading as a fort, all of it reminding her of the preening of men, peacocks with toys instead of wings. She sat next to the Commander, strange to be on his side of the desk, unsure if this was the normal spot for the guest chair. He smiled and his teeth were yellow, a feature that made you ignore his long thin face, protruding forehead, too-thin mustache the color of coconuts, a shade darker than his hair meticulously parted on the side.

"What can I do for you, Mr. Frank?" she asked.

"Call me Owen. You're not a soldier. No need to keep the formality when we are alone."

She should have bolted right then. *When we are alone*. Like this was the first of many solo visits to his office?

"So, you want to talk to me?" she asked cheerfully, trying to keep the tension she felt out of her voice.

"Yes, even though you are working as a civilian here we need to make sure everything is in order."

"I appreciate you taking care of my visa extension for me."

"Yes, well, we wouldn't want to be too hasty," he said. "I've had a private investigator do some digging and discovered your stage work."

"Just a way to make money for college."

"That you never finished," he said.

Heidi watched Owen's right hand reach out as though fumbling for an invisible drink. The bay window behind him rattled with the wind that rose at dusk. His hand, finally, settled on a fountain pen.

"I'd like to stay here."

"The question is how much? How much do you want me to sign this paperwork?"

She felt physically ill, resisting an image of the pen transforming into a gun. "Owen, I stand by my work with the dolphins. This decision is out of my hands."

She felt like a shadow had descended in the room and in times like these she imagined herself to be some mythic creature. In this case, a dragon. She could breathe a single word and roast Owen like a marshmallow the tourists loved to burn. Heidi rose to leave, but Owen's left hand shot out and pushed her down in her seat. Too shocked to move or speak, he grabbed her hand and held it over his crotch.

"I'm ready to sign but I'm looking for some inspiration."

What she considered doing next was no worse than what she'd done to men in the VIP room at a place called Club Paradise. It was a repetitive motion, and she could lose her mind on rebooting her life, on her relationship with Rick, on steeling herself to re-enter a normal life. This time felt different, though. She was aware of the power dynamics, the wolf beside her. The dragon fire almost, but not quite, ignited her darkest desires. Instead, she yanked her hand from Owen's grip above his crotch, his fingers leaving a red welt on her wrist.

She opened her mouth to speak but was stunned to see Owen signing her paperwork as if without a second thought. He gestured with a wave of his hand for her to leave. What the hell was that all about? Her face was crimson, and she felt like shrieking and pushing her foot into the bridge of his nose. But realizing that would only make a bad situation worse she turned to the door. She noticed it was open a crack and there—with eyes like lenses and a smile like a chasm in the earth that could swallow her whole—stood Clint Jenkins.

CHAPTER 2

Russell Copeland

RUSSELL STIRRED HIS VIRGIN MARGARITA from the poolside bar with a swizzle straw studded with miniature pirates. He was still a fan of umbrella drinks even without booze. Sobriety was not an escape from vice. The cigarette spuming in his hand confirmed his lack of commitment to addiction. Living on this remote caye made it impossible to squeeze scrips from his doctors. He, apparently, had spent his adulthood drawn to bad choices that kept wrecking him. He duck-walked in tan cargo shorts and a pair of worn leather sandals. An amble to the beach was his exercise, such as it was, to watch things happen. Smaller creatures scuttled and were eaten by larger ones. The losers washed up sometimes as jelly, sometimes as bones. Fossils hardened over time. He should know.

The warm breeze still stirred a smile after the previous four-and-change decades in Pittsburgh. He'd watched his father's ice business go under and found himself managing the properties the old man had left him. It took real skill to mistime the real estate market—to convert warehouses to lofts and office space right when the bottom dropped out. He was a trust fund wannabe who'd aged into a wreck of a man. His life carried flotsam like the crap that washed up on shore—a useless art history degree, an ex-wife Maxine and daughter Nancy who despised him, and a bankruptcy that had turned him into a junkie-in-training.

His redemption? His pops, the asshole, had died and left him with enough dough to start over. Of course, Russell had chosen real estate. In Belize. He sank all of his capital into a resort that had been damaged in a hurricane. What could go wrong? As it turned out, plenty. It has cost more than he'd thought to replace the damage to the twenty cabanas adjacent to a lagoon with a dazzling reef and bathtub warm surf. He'd been unaware the staff had been owed back wages, and he'd needed to make good on the former owner Quinn's debts. It had also cost him to brand the island *Copeland Caye* to match the new *Copeland Resort* sign above the lobby cum office overlooking the ping pong table where he occasionally held court.

What were the odds of a hurricane hitting the same spot again? Daniela Santos, his "kind-of" girlfriend and head of resort housekeeping, told him the island was called *Devil's Caye* by the locals. The island name had supposedly been spawned decades before in the ruined church nestled in the hundreds of acres of jungle inland. Locals had witnessed the cavalcade of Brits and Americans who had been driven off by maladies and tragedies over time. Though Russell had tried, Copeland Caye still hadn't been updated in Frommer's or even Google Maps. Could it be that he'd been swindled by his by-the-hour lawyer in Belize City who'd brokered the real estate deal? Too early to know. Besides, he had bigger fish to fry than even the ones caught by Brandon George, one half of the brother sister duo who ran the fishing charter and snorkeling boat for tourists. Barbara, his sister, called him *Boy George*. He returned the favor by calling his tomboy sister by the same moniker, so much so they were often referred to in the plural as *Boys George* or *Boy Georges*. They were also known to target the same tourist women for pick-ups and were ultra-competitive. Russell was grateful that the twins had decided to hang around the caye while he was running at half capacity, and at a financial loss.

This weekend would be a game changer. The ferry from the mainland would be carrying a wedding party, a private arrangement he'd brokered with Hollywood icon Wolf Granger. The director had booked all twelve cabanas for his daughter's wedding at a discount rate, promising word of mouth and to use the resort for a future film shoot if he made sure they had the island to themselves. Russell had agreed, of course, even though he had to outfit the supply hut with a bed and hasty decorations to accommodate the additional guests. He also hadn't mentioned that he only owned the south side of the caye. A mile northeast through the jungle was the collection of huts called D-town where a small community of Belizeans lived. Almost all of the residents worked at the resort or were employed by the boats, except for the bar Cava just a couple minutes' walk down the beach and a convenience store called D-stop—owned by the locals. To the west was the US Navy SEAL training center, rumored to be where elite teams learned advanced munitions. This mini fortress was rumored to be where the elite teams learned advanced munitions. Cliffs ringed the caye's eastern side with a private beach that only the natives knew how to get to except for the occasional tourist spelunking. Brandon pissed off the locals by jetting his fishing expeditions through a passage in the reef onto this beach to cook up fresh snappers at sunset over an open fire. The tension among the three groups here was palpable but manageable most of the time. Russell wasn't about to let anything go wrong this weekend.

The ferry was taking its time navigating its way through the shallows toward the resort's dock. Russell felt unusually anxious and decided to leave instead of pacing in front of his new guests. He didn't want to make the wrong first impression. He radioed for Daniela to send several of the maids down to the pier to help the guests orient themselves. They had no bellhop— he was the only man at the resort. His girlfriend told him that he must enjoy being surrounded by a *coven*. When he tried to correct her by telling her it was a *harem* she had laughed at the bravado. Even when he thought he was the one in charge the women in his life could see right through him.

He tried to keep his inner perfectionist at bay on his walk back along the cobblestone paths a previous owner from London had imported. Alongside the path was a bed of wildflowers, a once orderly planting that ended up in a flurry of competing colors. Orange, red, and pink petals intermixed in dazzling swirls. Daniela had told him the names of the plants countless times, but he'd lost the ability, seemingly, to hold them in his head. The effect was like abstract art, a passion of his. His mother had worried his fussiness made him less than a man. He was metrosexual before it even had a name. His ex-wife had let him know that his finances weren't the only reason she'd left him. He had desires for women like he had for many beautiful things. The animal urge in him was buried unless he was wasted, and then impossible for him to control. His addiction to booze had come with one to porn.

Keeping himself busy was one answer. Preparation for this relaunch of Copeland Resort had helped him keep his demons at bay. The rebuild of the cabanas post-storm had allowed him to put his own touches everywhere. Planters and decorative stones. Local artwork and more windows framing beach and forest vistas. This resort felt like an extension of himself, and he was sensitive to its success in ways he hadn't felt in decades. There was a lot riding on this wedding party, not just economically. He was overexposed emotionally as well. One thing he hadn't gotten to yet was the border of his property ringed with palm trees, once manicured but now overgrown, that gave definition to his property and the jungle beyond. Well, there would always be something that needed work.

He came out of his stupor and nodded at Daniela stationed behind the front desk. He'd been having a difficult time sleeping, even after being diagnosed with apnea and given a machine that wheezed and a mask to don at night. He wasn't sure if it was working as intended—the physician who'd recommended it was back in Pittsburgh. He hadn't gotten used to sleeping on his back, that was part of the problem. The other was his vanity. He didn't want Daniela, young enough to be his daughter, to think of him as an old man. So, he didn't always turn the machine on in case it would turn her off. His fatigue was now a part of him, it seemed. He spaced out far too often.

His gaze was drawn to the brightly colored walls beside the open door, painted the color of lemons, just as the outsides of the buildings were the hue of lime. He looked at a portrait hung above a cabinet where they kept slices of fresh guava and coconut. He'd bought it from their resident painter on this island, Enrique. The artist was a Bohemian among his fellow islanders, barefoot, with a scraggly goatee. The frame was inexpensive sandalwood, and the medium was acrylic. The man in the portrait was alone, seated in a hotel lobby much like this one, seething about something. He was nude but his posture concealed his genitals, and he gripped a corncob pipe like a gun, pointing it at the audience. If you studied his skin, you could see multiple layers, as though the artist took many attempts to get the color right. As a result, the man protruded nearly a half-inch from the canvas.

So intent was Russell on this image that he didn't notice another person slide into the doorway. A woman jangled from too much jewelry and her scent was a mixture of flowers and ash, perfume and smoke, as familiar as hell.

"You sure are living pretty down here," said Maxine, his ex-wife.

Inwardly freaking out. Russell was able to respond matter-of-factly, "There's no room for you here. Every room's filled with a wedding party."

"No worries, I'll sleep in your bed."

Maxine smiled and swung her shoulder-length red hair, bridled in a ponytail, so that it snapped around like a scorpion's tail.

"The hell you will," Daniela said, popping up out of her chair, her face the level of Maxine's breasts.

The awkward silence bloomed into an almost human presence. There would be hell to pay, Russell had no doubt. He just didn't know what form that hell would take. A gust whipped in from the ocean, wiping away his wife's scent with the fecund smell of paradise lost then found.

"Whoa... now where's my camera?" a confident voice boomed through a thick brown beard on a tall, thin white man with not a hair on his head. He ate up the floor with long strides, his half-unbuttoned white shirt draping over khakis, brown chest hair fluttering, gray eyes cresting above rose-colored tortoise-shell glasses.

Russell recognized him on sight, probably from some award show or another. So did Maxine, who'd always blamed him for keeping her from being a famous actress, for holding her talents hostage in the Pittsburgh community theater scene.

"Wolf Granger, welcome to Copeland Resort. I'm Maxine Copeland."

"And she is trespassing," Daniela said.

"My ex-wife," Russell stammered.

"I love drama in all of its forms but not during my daughter's wedding," Wolf said, launching a thumb backward toward a caravan of approaching guests.

Wheeled luggage clacked toward the hotel lobby cabana. Russell almost burst out of the lobby to greet them, then spun to see if he might need to break up the impending wrestling match between his girlfriend and ex-wife, before whirling in a three-hundred-and-sixty-degree tilt, slightly dizzy and facing Wolf.

"Quit acting like a cartoon character and get my family checked in," Wolf said.

Russell hit the knob on the bell, hoping some of the maids would pitch in with the bags after hearing a *ding* drifting across the resort. Daniela stomped back behind the front desk and muttered in a low angry voice, "Next."

Margarita, the largest of the maids, with broad shoulders and a warm smile, arrived in the lobby. Russell waved her over and she began separating luggage from the first wave of visitors. Maxine smiled like she had won some minor victory and Russell felt stuck in a trap of his own making.

Nothing escaped the director's smoky eyes. Wolf ran thick fingers, like sausages, through his beard and muttered, "Things better go as planned."

This is always the hope, but it rarely does, Russell thought before clearing his throat and saying, "Yes, sir."

Chapter 3

Marley Vega

MARLEY VEGA ALWAYS SUSPECTED THAT his name was cooler than he was…and he was pretty damn cool for a seventeen-year-old. Marley had been a family name, the moniker of a great-grandfather who'd graduated from piracy to becoming, if not a respectable businessman, then at least a wealthy one. Marley tried to listen to Bob Marley, at times, and the music spoke to him the way sunlight spoke to a vampire. He had too much darkness in his heart to sway with reggae. There must be a reason behind the shadow worlds he inhabited. He penned mean-spirited poetry that took swipes at enemies real and imagined: corporations, aristocrats, his father. His voodoo poetry was sometimes peppered with post-apocalyptic streams of thought painting grim, alternate realities. He wasn't *depressed*, as his mother, vacationing in Paris, claimed. He just hadn't had to choose a side yet in the many battles, large and small, swimming around him.

It was dusk, his favorite time on Devil's Caye. He refused to call it Copeland Caye, even if the dude who ran the resort was harmless, as far as Americans went. Marley was precocious, for many reasons, the least of which was finishing his freshman year abroad at UC Berkeley. His father Gibraltar was a cabinet member and Minister of Works, Transport, and the

National Emergency Management Organization (NEMO). Marley kidded that his father loved his job for how easy it was to siphon cash from an organization that had its fingers in far too many things. His father smiled at these jibes and was fully committed to him, at least committed to sending him away from home as much as possible. So, Gibraltar parked him on Devil's Caye with a summer job helping his Grandpapi Rex run his bar, Cava. Truth was that he didn't mind hanging with the old coot. He suspected he was planted here because his father was embarrassed by him, at least the aspect of himself that was more-or-less openly gay.

Gibraltar had only himself to blame. Marley had more in common with rich kids all over the world than he did with the Belizeans in D-town, the stretch of beach on the northwest side of the caye. His school year in Berkeley had been the best of his life, even if it was difficult to convince other guys to date him with the age difference and worries about the American legal system. Marley had been a chameleon his entire school year abroad: fraternity pledge, intramural fencing enthusiast, drama club extra, pot smoker, regular at local venues for stand-up mic nights. His poetry was word salad, sometimes vitriolic and at other times a stew of misery meets anger. His dorm roomie Derrick was a nice-enough Midwest guy and he felt bad pushing the boundaries of his acceptance by inviting over the weirdest of the Berkeley weird to hang in their room. Unlike his father, Derrick had an endless reservoir of acceptance, or at least politeness. They developed an odd-couple bond that felt as real as anything else in his life.

"Marley," Grandpapi called down the stairs to Cava's basement, and he pretended not to hear him. He was doodling in his notebook instead of rooting around for a case of Red Stripe, one of the six beers served in the bar. He had squirreled a chair down in the basement and used a desk fashioned from three empty cases of Negro Modelo. The lighting was dim from a single bulb, the chain swinging above his head as though from a ghost or some impossible breeze. He kept a library of a half-dozen poetry books on a windowsill covered by dirt, having just read the Lorca classic *Poet in New York*. His own mission was not to see the world through the eyes of an outsider like Lorca. He was attempting to reclaim a place, a Belize that he had been walled off from. He wasn't happy, yet, with the first two lines of his poem:

The roots of a dying tree push through the cellar,
seeking a wet place, buried, like my own cock.

He was a damned cliché, trying to find his roots. Literally. He was angry about growing up in the ultra-wealthy Fort George neighborhood in Belize City. It was originally an island that developers had connected to the rest of the city with landfill and garbage. A bridge of refuse. He was ashamed of his years abroad in boarding schools—London, Paris, Madrid. He was as much an outsider in D-town as the damned tourists. He tried to blend in, but he was a lost cause in every way imaginable. His only friend was his grandfather Rex, a man who said and did what he wanted... but in exile. Rumor had it that his grandfather had once been the head of a crime family but had laundered his money into a string of bars. Gibraltar had reportedly "retired" him from the family business before going "legit" as a politician, a career that gave him the pull to help out his old associates in new ways.

"Marley, get your ass up here," Rex called down again, this time with agitation, but not urgency. His grandfather was never stressed out, not on an island like this, surrounded by soft tourists and American sailors. None of them had been in the battles he had and lived to tell the tale, or so he always said.

Marley, on the other hand, felt something sinister behind doors, around the corner, in the jungle. He touched the scar funneling down his eye to cheek, the remnant of a dog's bite, one of their family's pets and guard dog. He barely remembered the stitches and being carried into the car and to the hospital. The dog was put to sleep, and he'd been left with a fear of all animals, including humans. Even now, he could hear the squeals of the spider monkeys in the trees, and he imagined them wanting to tear him apart.

Marley unlocked the gate and stepped into a former jail cell converted to house the liquor and food for the bar. He would be lying if he hadn't thought what it would be like to accidentally be locked inside, without the key he kept around this neck all last year at school, partly a Bohemian fashion statement and partially a reminder of his love for his grandfather. He picked up a case of Red Stripe, careful to make sure the cardboard bottom hadn't rotted through. He was able to lock up again without setting down his haul and strained to

21

climb the steep stairs. He emerged into the bar's kitchen. It was basically just a tiny alcove with a toaster oven, microwave, and pantry. He occasionally whipped up a few on-the-fly snacks for their drunken patrons just like he had for his fraternity bros after too many brewskis.

He paused for a moment to gather in the view from the kitchen window overlooking the patio. It was sunset and the light flickered over the treetops, pulsating with the calls of the birds and monkeys in the hundreds of acres of jungle separating the triangular points of the island: resort, SEAL base, D-town. The beach curved from D-town to the naval base and from the base to the resort. The shoreline dead-ended to the east, blocked by boulders and rising to cliffs that covered the eastern jut of the island. Fissures and caves dug below the cliffs and were supposedly off-limits to the tourists, who seemed to wander into them far too often. The locals knew a path through the caverns leading to Angel Beach. This was a white sand haven that the locals tried to keep for themselves, and the tourists kept visiting on their fishing tours. The locals had cut a few paths through the jungle and some of the resort guests would make their way through the brush to D-town, featuring a small convenience store and a few carts selling trinkets.

Marley stepped out of the kitchen into the bustling bar and adjusted his eyes to the dim lighting. Cava extended out from a circular bar well. The design of the building was like a flower, expanded over decades of carpentry and intermittent storm repairs. The bulbous walls made you feel inebriated the moment you stepped inside.

The bar was the largest structure on the island outside of the abandoned church in the middle of the rainforest. A series of hastily erected additions extended the bar to the edge of the beach in one direction, to the resort in another, and to the forest path leading to D-town. The pod-like layout provided three sections where the locals, tourists, and sailors kept to themselves. The bar patrons occasionally intermingled in a fourth section next to a large-screen TV.

The broadcast bounced in dizzying fashion around the bar from a series of mirrors on the walls. The décor was anything but classic island tourist. Rex had decorated it with the sophisticated artwork and filled bookshelves from his former home in Belize City. It gave the establishment more of a lodge or cabin feel.

"About time," Rex said, and motioned for Marley to fill up one of the half-dozen mini fridges beneath the bar.

Even though it was still early, there was a group of tourists, some young, some old, getting tanked and chatting with increasing volume. It looked like Russell had finally roped in the wedding party he'd been ranting about the entire summer.

Marley thought of Cava as almost an extension of the resort as a cobblestone path between the two was just a stone's throw away from the swimming pool. Rex would have bristled at this. Grandpapi was his own man and owed his loyalty to himself and his family. Russell was much more deferential to Rex than the previous resort owner, Quinn, who'd been batshit crazy.

The current resort owner was at his usual table, drinking a club soda, his girlfriend Daniela on one side and a tall buxom redhead on the other. These women stared each other down and held onto Russell's arms as though about to snap him in two to make a wish. There were only two sailors in the joint tonight. On the weekends the trainees got shore leave, the SEALs only came in by the handful. Rick sat with his girlfriend Heidi, the dolphin trainer. They were both regulars and a good couple, if Marley could be the judge of such things. A SEAL trainee he didn't know was getting plowed and scowling at the soccer game between Mexico and Costa Rica that Rex had selected from the thousands of choices on the satellite TV.

Grandpapi played whatever he liked, whenever he liked. Occasionally, one of the guests tried to bully him into another sporting event or thought he was someone to pour their hearts out to and get sympathy. He was venomous in his advice and unyielding in his observations. He carried the air of a former mobster long after his son had put him out to pasture to clean up the family name. He was a real bastard, and everyone seemed to love him for it. And now he was giving Marley the evil eye. *Fine*, said Marley under his breath, picking up the drink tickets, and started delivering the orders.

He lived for the gossip, for the lives of the other people on the island since his was so empty. He considered the regular clientele as close to friends as he would manage this summer. Tonight, it was hopping so he was too busy to stop and chat. His first stop was a double rum and Coke for Jira Santos, the D-stop owner and Daniela's uncle. He had shoulder-length gray hair and a tattoo of a devil on his shoulder, one that was green instead of red, a jungle demon. These two didn't speak often, unlike the Boys George, the heavily tanned twins, already hammered and playing a rowdy game of rock, paper, scissors in the corner.

Next up was a third margarita for Heidi, the dolphin trainer, not usually a heavy drinker. She was whispering to Rick, her forehead rubbing his brawny shoulder. She held her drink with both hands and looked as though she was going to worship it like an ancient island artifact before pushing the straw into her mouth. Rick's face was redder than the crimson trim of the super-gay Belize flag, which depicted a shirtless boy holding an axe next to a slightly darker boy gripping a paddle. Marley had always thought the image was evocative, perhaps an early sign he was gay. The only place the Belize flag flew on the caye was next to the American flag, visible over the walls of the SEAL compound.

Marley's last delivery was a Red Stripe ordered by the trainee. The dude was barely older than him and had one of those faces that made it seem like he was making fun of you and the world. Perhaps Marley was being oversensitive. He set down the beer and was about to settle the tab when the SEAL jumped to his feet. Marley could hear heavy boots stomping toward him from behind. He stepped sideways to avoid a freight train—Heidi's boyfriend approached the table and glared at the trainee.

"Clint, you didn't finish cleaning your kit. What the hell are you doing here?" Rick asked.

"I'm hanging out in this crappy bar. Looks like I'm surrounded by dumbass civilians while all my friends are picking up babes on the mainland," Clint said.

"You're on this island because you can't seem to follow orders. Go home. It's a public service to not have you getting drunk and harassing women."

"You think I harass women? You're blind, dude. I have a story I think you're going to want to hear." Clint's thin face had a few wispy whiskers of red hair on his chin like a baby goat.

"Clint, shut your face," Heidi called out from across the bar, still gripping

24

the margarita like a religious artifact but with the liquid now half gone.

"Yeah, baby," Clint said, giving a mock salute with his beer hand and sloshing beer over his shoulder in the process. The foam splashed the face of Jira passing by to use the bathroom.

The D-stop owner reacted instantly—he shoved Clint so hard that he rammed into a bald man in khaki shorts and white dress shirt who'd just entered the bar.

As the bald man fell backward, he flailed and caught the tail of Clint's shirt as the trainee ricocheted and grabbed Jira's hands. It was like a demented conga line, comical at first with the tourist's momentum driving the threesome toward the door.

"I'm the father of the bride, dammit," the tourist cried out. "I paid for this whole island."

"It's our island," Jira snapped, enraged, driving himself into Clint to reach for the bald man's throat on the other side. They were now a whirling, six-armed, six-legged beast, bumping into tables and spinning out the door.

This was a disaster in the making. Marley wasn't sure what to do as Cava emptied out into a small courtyard with benches, ashtrays, and decorative totems. Heidi's boyfriend Rick was the only one, seemingly, with a plan. The SEAL marched outside and planted his fist into the other sailor's mouth, stepped on one of Wolf's dress shoes, and tugged on the back of Jira's head with a fistful of white hair.

"Everyone calm the hell down," Rick barked.

Rex rushed out of the bar with a cricket bat and gripped Marley's shoulder, pulling him back out of the press of bodies. Marley glanced at Grandpapi and then back at Rick, who stood like a statue with fist cocked.

Marley almost missed it. The nearly full moon glowed over the sailor's hand. An object streaked toward it, a shooting star, a rocket, an asteroid. The finger of some alien god. A silent explosion seemed to leap up from Rick's fist. The moon absorbed the missile. For a moment. Then, the familiar silver orb belched out a mushroom cloud, visible even at dusk.

"The MOON!" Marley bellowed, thrusting his arm skyward and jabbing a finger at the unfolding scene. The crowd turned, looked towards the moon, and fell silent...tourists, locals, military alike. Something terrible had happened and was still happening. The moon was spitting out parts of itself, just as Clint was spitting blood from his mouth. The sky was shimmering with shards of lunar debris. Words could not explain the tragedy. Nothing would ever be the same.

CHAPTER 4

Russell Copeland

RUSSELL GAVE UP ON SLEEP around four AM or did it give up on him? He wasn't sure whether his insomnia was related to him giving up his cabana to his ex-wife, an incident that had prompted a fight with Daniela, and sent her packing back to her hut in D-town. Perhaps it was the excitement of the near brawl at Cava, and the threats of Wolf Granger to fly his party to the Atlantis resort for some real Caribbean ambience. More likely, it was the dramatic impact of the asteroid to the moon that had made him fearful of a multitude of world-ending scenarios. All he knew was that his former go-to for stress from his past life—boozing it up—was no longer available to him. It also didn't help that he'd crammed an uncomfortable cot into the scuba rental shack that he loaned out to the Georges, located just behind the swimming pool and within view of the Cava Bar.

He strolled to the edge of the resort, lit a cigarette, and meandered down the path to the beach. He was surprised to discover he was not the only one awake. Wolf Granger, smart phone in hand, filmed the sky while occasionally tugging on the end of a bottle. Probably rum. Russell felt the walkway end and his sandaled feet plopped themselves into sand. The Hollywood director looked like a creature that may have climbed up out of the sea, except the

27

water had receded nearly to the reef. What the hell? The tide line was a hundred feet beyond anything he'd ever seen. The hairs on the back of his neck stood on end. He felt the tingle of a panic attack and tried to think of the positives. The temperature was still a balmy 80 degrees, the same day and night, and he admired the consistency. The sand was cool on his toes, and he wiggled them. Don't think about the damn tide. Don't think about the ex-wife and the dual desire to bed her and send her packing. Definitely don't think about downing a drink, toking a reefer, inhaling a line.

"Been filming the moon," Wolf said, his vowels slurring into consonants. "And it's still there."

"Not even an asteroid can knock it out of the sky I guess," Russell said.

"Exactly. Better the moon gets smacked around than us. This is what we get, huh, for leaving America?"

Russell opened his mouth, wondering what the hell the director was getting at. There was nothing about being in the US that made a natural disaster like this any better or worse. Maybe he was referring to his involvement in the fight, such as it was. In the cabanas along his property, Russell could see that there were lights on in nearly all of them, everything and everyone thrown off kilter from the evening's events. He needed to get his act together. He was the one expected to play host, to make his guest feel better, even if Wolf was a world-class jerk. Atlantis? Jesus. The sunrise was beginning to lighten the sky, to dim the presence of the damaged moon peering down on them.

"C'mon, what we both need is a cup of Java. They have the best at Cava," Russell said.

"You're a god-damn poet. That rhymes, you know?"

Wolf laughed and Russell wondered if he, too, thought himself that funny when he drank copiously for so many years among acquaintances long since forgotten. His own specialty had been the pun, and these still occasionally launched from his mouth and generally landed awkwardly out into the world. Daniela snickered at them all, and he knew that he was a lucky man. When women did this, he assumed they enjoyed the man as much as the conversation. And now that he'd kicked her out of his cabana, their relationship was on the rocks (another drinking reference). What the hell was wrong with him?

"My own damn daughter is pissed at me. Can you believe that?" Wolf asked. "It wasn't as though that lame-ass fight was my fault."

What Russell wanted to say: *It never is, is it?* What Russell actually said: "I couldn't be sorrier for last night. Really, this place is a paradise. We're much more civilized than this."

Wolf looked Russell up and down with doubtful eyes and a smug grin.

Russell nodded and began striding down the beach, trying to punish the drunk Hollywood director with a quick pace. Surprisingly, Wolf kept stride with him easily as they trundled toward the silhouette of Cava. The roiling of the waves echoed in the distance and the air was saturated with salt. Russell could feel the tiredness in his calves, the sand weighing him down. The sprawling building was leaking light out its windows and open doors. Rex was always awake before him. He wasn't sure the old man really slept, and the door to the bar was usually open at sunrise. In this case, before.

Inside Cava, it soon became clear how much things were different and the same in the rest of the world. Rex and his grandson Marley nursed cups of coffee and were watching the large-screen TV. The news was on, and they mirrored each other soundlessly, in the dips of cups to lips, closeness without words. Russell and his daughter used to read the news, from various sources, across from one another over breakfast. This was a shared trait that made her flittering mother crazy, scraping plates in the kitchen while they meandered through the start of their day. The banner beneath a male and female reporter read: *Sleep Patterns Disturbed Worldwide: Is the Asteroid Moon Collision to Blame?*

"Feel free to serve yourself coffee," Rex said, gesturing over his shoulder with a flick of his head. "Did either of you sleep?"

"Not a wink," Wolf said with a wink and a face eager for someone to acknowledge his cleverness.

"What's going on?" Russell asked, while Wolf sauntered over to the bar and set two large black mugs on the counter.

"Apparently, some scientists believe the shift in tides from the moon being pushed into a different orbit affected our sleep," Marley said.

"We're living in a dream now," Rex said. "At least, our days will seem like dreams."

"Hope you like your coffee black."

"That's fine," Russell said, but it wasn't, not with the specter of sleeplessness facing them all.

"I'm sure we're all just shaken up by what we saw. We'll get used to the change," Wolf said.

Russell settled into a chair, watching a scientist talking head who looked ragged, tired, and scared. The Hollywood director soon joined him and set down one of the mugs in front of him. The steam from the cup felt like the breath of a woman, and he'd never been able to sleep well without one by his side. His prognosis of sleep apnea, the month before he left the U.S., had provided him with a pervasive sense of dread and a machine that he only occasionally used. It wasn't just the slurping sound reminiscent of people on life support. When he wore the mask, it felt like an alien force breathing into his nostrils, an invasion of air. No wonder he was tired. He took a careful sip of coffee and tasted the whiskey there, the old demon hiding in the blackness.

"You're welcome," Wolf said with a self-satisfied smirk.

"Don't you know I...." Russell paused, trying to slow the heartbeat pounding in his chest. "I'm going to do everything I can for you and the wedding party."

"That's the spirit, champ."

"I'm not sure the wedding's going to happen," Marley said.

Wolf whirled to face the kid, his mouth ready to explode. Russell readied himself for, well, anything, and took a second sip of coffee. Instead, Wolf paused and followed Marley's line of sight toward the resort dock. The George twins' boat, *Georgeous,* puttered up to dock from its customary spot of being anchored offshore. After dark, it was a party boat, where many guests ended up in one or the other George's bed, occasionally both.

Russell squinted and a topless woman appeared on deck. She sidled up to Brandon piloting the boat while his sister Barbara jumped onto the dock and secured the boat.

"I'll be damned," Wolf said. "Here comes the bride. The walk of shame to end all walk of shames."

"The moon is to blame," Rex said, making the mark of horns with two fingers to ward off evil spirits.

"What happens in Belize…" Russell started to joke but the words escaped him even as the alcohol warmed his insides and dulled his senses. He needed to stop telling himself this was just coffee.

"This is what my future son-in-law Trevor deserves. He didn't let Kara have a bachelorette party—looks like she's showing him who's in charge."

"That's some messed-up shit," Marley said.

Unabashedly, Wolf picked up his camera and started filming his daughter pulling her swimsuit top back on and giving each of the George siblings a more-than-friendly kiss. Brother and sister both had short blond hair and gave each other a high five after Kara stepped down carefully onto the dock. Russell recognized her—he was surprised he hadn't pieced it together before. She was a model and minor celebrity in her own right. Kara wobbled, seemingly as drunk as her father, toward the ocean-side entrance of Cava.

"The White House doesn't have any comment, but some want to declare martial law. It's not safe to drive or to fly until we understand this better. You can survive for days without sleep but not without a radical shift in behavior."

Russell turned to the television while another expert droned on about the crisis. Rex looked at his hands as though there might be an extra finger hidden in plain sight. Kara Granger slipped into the bar and her doting father quickly hooked her up with his special coffee. Russell's was almost finished. *No rest for the wicked.* That was a saying. In this case, it was a prophecy.

CHAPTER 5

Heidi Radar

HEIDI CLIMBED OUT OF BED in the pre-dawn hours feeling the absence of her boyfriend…and something more perhaps. Rick had decided to hit the gym. His was one of the few private rooms in the mansion converted to barracks but she still felt uneasy here. She took a shower to try to reclaim her senses and slowly got dressed. They'd had sex twice with the wounded moon framed in his barred window, but nothing had done the trick to put them to sleep. This was unusual…at least for Rick. Her beefcake normally slept like a champ.

Rick had decided that exercise was his ticket to slumber. With the temperatures holding close to 80 degrees Fahrenheit, day or night, it was never too hot for physical exertion. His theory, not hers. Heidi was a veteran of staying up all night, for various reasons. When she'd worked as an exotic dancer, she saw the light pop up over the ocean from many vantage points and stages of inebriation. These travels through the underbelly of Los Angeles were almost never planned and they usually involved a stranger or two, sometimes another dancer or two.

Heidi had yet to live up to the clairvoyance of her last name Radar. In fact, she stumbled through most situations with a knack for doing the most damage to herself. She trudged through the SEAL living quarters with a heavy heart and footsteps. She felt doom fluttering in the molting darkness and listened to the waves whooshing in the distance. She stepped outside to the docks covered with a corrugated tin roof and slipped off her sandals, making her way to a row of lockers pressed against the building. She breathed in deeply, stretched her back and shoulders, and practiced a sloppy yoga on the concrete.

It had always been clear she had no "safe space" to meditate. Not here. Not ever. She rose and gathered a few flotation devices from the supply locker and hauled them over to the dolphin pens. She set up a makeshift mattress next to the water and watched Flo and Jet swim in circles, chirping to her. The dolphin tank was where she felt most comfortable, without a need to explain who the hell she was or how she got here. Her expiring visa and credentials didn't matter to these creatures. The dolphins were verbose this morning. She could sense that they were trying to tell her something. She didn't have the language for it. Her head felt like it was two sizes too big and throbbed like it had received a punch as strong as the asteroid to the moon.

Before bed, she'd scanned the news headlines to make sure there was nothing disastrous in motion like a tidal wave that would wipe them all out. Nothing popped on her phone on the "fake news" sites she liked to surf, although their slow internet access was even slower than usual. The ocean sounded different, tinnier, something. A klaxon for the pent-up dolphins. Something was telling her that she should be frightened, and she obliged, waiting for the sun to sink like a stone.

Her foreboding hadn't dissipated later when she wandered up the beach to Cava. After breakfast washed down with endless coffee all anyone could talk about was the collective state of insomnia. The bar swelled with hotel guests and locals from D-town. Even Owen, the SEAL Commander, had trekked over to grab a cup of Joe and share in the gossip with Rex and his grandson. Heidi refused to listen to the pundits on the TV or in bathing suits. The conversations among customers oscillated between light alarm and conspiracy theories.

Heidi was certain the world was ending. She knew that without proper REM you went mad. Perhaps, because so many things had gone wrong in her life, it was easy for her to imagine the worst-case scenario. She'd once stayed up for five days with one of her boyfriends, a DJ who spun in the strip club she worked at. He'd gotten a batch of meth for payment in lieu of cash and they hadn't seen any reason not to party. By the end, both of them were seeing ghosts. She saw her grandparents sitting at times in her room and, eventually, her boyfriend as a translucent angel-in-waiting. Luckily, their stash ran out or things may have progressed to an even more dire state.

Rick, used to an orderly world, had been agitated. He took his 'bad attitude' trainee Clint on a version of a mud run, twice around the island. She saw them lap the bar with Rick pushing the pace to punish the dumb shit. She felt adrift with no naval exercises today and had already fed the dolphins. The best thing to do would be to distract herself with the tourists—an activity she excelled at. She was sick of the pool, ping pong tables, and the beach sand sticking in every crack hours after a shower. She wanted to get away from her fretting, even for a little while, and decided to throw her lot in with the Boys George.

Unfortunately, drama followed her out to the charter boat *Georgeous*, but in a different form. The charter carried the parents of the bride and groom on a fishing expedition, and there was conflict to be sure. Apparently, if the mothers of the bride and groom were any indication, they both blamed the same person: Kara. Heidi tried hard to stare out at the waves, imagining herself to be a mermaid, more powerful in this transient realm between sea and land. A creature with the ability to drown sailors or to save them from themselves. She imagined a second row of teeth, like a shark's, that would extend if she ever felt like snapping.

On the surface, the day seemed like any other—blue sky and aquamarine water with visibility down to the red reef that rippled below the surface like the blood of the sea. The wind swept through Heidi's hair. The salt licked her skin and burrowed into her scalp. It felt like some otherworldly power was trying to bore into her like all the men in her life. Jesus, she was just tweaking. Fatigue was starting to settle in, and she caught snatches of conversation like it was coming in on a faraway radio frequency. She began to question the judgment of the Boys George for heading out with unknown tidal shifts and her own judgment for tagging along.

34

"Kara is acting out because she doesn't like that I married her father," Jewel Granger said.

She wasn't much older than her stepdaughter and Heidi couldn't help but wonder if she hadn't been a model or actress, the bait that Hollywood types seemed to devour like endless chum. It was then she noticed the name Jewel embroidered on her shawl and it became clear that she was a brand all in herself, just like Wolf Granger. How did a woman with a porn star's name and a capitalist's heart end up with her in the same boat, nipples pointing at the invisible broken moon?

"Trevor should give her a piece of his mind, Liza Keith curtly replied. "He lets Kara walk all over him." The mother of the groom was wearing a fluffy white bathrobe over her two-piece black swimsuit with "Copeland" embroidered into the sleeves. The resort owner had cranked out various keepsakes like this that he sold after the fact for one hundred bucks a pop. "I didn't spend all of the time homeschooling him to have him turn into a...."

"Mama's boy?" Jewel asked.

"I was going to say pussy, but I didn't want to be rude," Liza said.

"You're in the wrong wedding for that, sister. Don't cry now."

"Not sure why my eyes won't stop watering. Probably just from getting no sleep. I won't shed a tear over that slut of yours."

Jewel shrugged and thought better of a reply. The aroma of bait drifted over from the stern of the boat as the fathers of the bride and groom fished with Brandon George while Barbara sunbathed on the deck. Brother and sister were androgynous and enticing. Heidi could sense the scent of sex laced in the wind, or perhaps it was the mermaid inside of her responding to a desire she shouldn't consummate.

"If Trevor's such a mama's boy then maybe I should tell him to leave Kara at the altar," Jewel said.

"It would be the best thing for the girl. Only I don't think he's got the nerve."

"You think Trevor is wrapped around her finger?" Liza asked, dabbing her eyes with a handkerchief. "Jesus, you're probably right."

Jewel snorted and opened a beer from the cooler next to her. It was already her third. "I don't think Kara is ready to commit to anyone. She's a narcissist like her father."

"I'm not a prude but cheating on my son…in a threesome? It's too much."

"But you couldn't keep yourself from coming along, could you?" Jewel asked. "You had to see what the fuss was about." Her voice dropped to a whisper. "Who the fuss was about."

"There are more delicious things than the fish on this boat. That's for sure." Liza said.

"It's why I came. Maybe you two want a threesome with me?" Heidi asked flirtatiously. She wasn't sure why she was being so immature. She thought she'd long ago graduated from fucking with people just for the shock value, but it was as though the lack of sleep had stripped away the years, bringing her closer to the wounds that she normally so carefully hid away.

The two women huddled close together even as they looked at her wordlessly. Shock registered on their faces. Maybe Heidi would help them understand they were allies in this world of men holding all the cards. When cosmic forces like the moon are thrown into chaos women start to feel their true power. Or perhaps they were all beginning to lose their minds.

"I'd take you up on that for sure," Barbara said, shifting onto her side, her breasts bouncing with the waves.

"I got one," Wolf whooped, and the tension was broken. For now, at least.

Simon Keith, the tall thin father of the groom, looked pissed that he hadn't nabbed the first score, and recast his line. The "mothers" in the wedding party got up, but not before shooting Heidi dirty looks, and headed over to the stern of the boat to see what the fuss was about.

In all, the men managed to haul in three red snappers, the size of Chihuahuas, and Brandon maneuvered them into a cove on the far side of the island to eat lunch. *Angel Beach* was the name of it, the one place of purity on Devil's Caye, even more than the abandoned church in the middle of the jungle. At Cava, she'd heard stories of how the children of the islanders were baptized there and it was not a journey any of them took lightly. They did not picnic or surf there and expected tourists to follow suit.

The locals on the island knew a way to get to the beach through a circuit of caves that were dangerous, confusing, and apparently off limits. This did not, however, stop the resort fishing boat from maneuvering close enough for them to anchor and paddle over to the small clearing with palm and coconut trees providing shade for a strip of white sand beach. Brandon carried a chest that contained their fresh fish on ice, the handle of a machete sticking out of it. Barbara carried the beer cooler pressed to her head like it was a boom box, and only she could groove to the beat of cans sloshing in ice water. Heidi swam ahead and came up out of the water like a mermaid with new legs and a regal air. The two older couples brought up the rear, first the menfolk, pleased to have caught what would be an early dinner. Then the women followed without robes, hats, or shawls, the differences in income or social status less visible dripping from the ocean and strolling onto shore.

The Boys George led them over to a fire pit surrounded by logs as makeshift seats. There was already firewood ready to go set above a pit of stones, with a grill on top of it. This was obviously not the first time they'd taken a charter over to cook "fresh" fish. Heidi's mermaid aura seemed to be failing this far onshore, and her confidence in coming along on this trip dissipated as quickly as the breeze off the ocean. She looked at the two couples, and brother and sister and felt panic rising within her. It was more than just feeling like a seventh wheel (was there such a thing?). Black smoke rose like the fingers of a demon from the fish charring on the grill. Time passed in chunks, like the spokes of a tire. A couple of tomatoes had been tossed onto the grill and the smell was intoxicating even as the smoke encircled them. Was she imaging the vortex opening beneath the flames? She blinked and looked away toward the small grove of trees beside them, trying to regain her composure.

Brandon emerged from behind a tree with a coconut in his hand and gave her a wink. He tossed it from hand to hand like a slow-witted juggler. His calves bulged as he crossed the white sand to the fire pit.

"Nothing like fresh fruit," Barbara said, flipping their fish by the tail on the grill, her back to her brother.

"Or a fresh kill," Brandon replied, placing the coconut on a flat rock next to the cooler.

"I'm hungry," Heidi found herself saying, and the nods from the older couples on either side of her proved that she'd spoken the words out loud.

She was so beat that she was having a hard time distinguishing what she thought and what she said.

Brandon steadied the enormous coconut with his left hand and his right hand gripped the machete by a handle that had been wrapped with electrical tape. Everyone turned to watch him as he ceremoniously lifted the blade over his head.

"This is our beach!" A voice cried out from a cave overlooking the cove, cut into the cliff twenty feet above them. Jira, owner of the D-stop and vocal leader of the locals, shook his fist and cackled loudly. "*Putas*, go to hell!"

Barbara jumped up, shaking her fist. "You don't scare me you pathetic, old man! Come down here and I'll beat you like a drum."

"It's too late for you. You're already dead."

Behind them the machete landed with a thwack and there was a gasping sound, part animal, part human. Barbara reached over to grab a piece of the coconut, threatening to throw it at their tormenter. Red juice trickled down her forearm. Arm cocked, she realized that what she gripped was actually a human hand cut off at the wrist. Beside her, Brandon swayed on the balls of his feet, in shock, the coconut intact. Blood spurted from his stump, splashing into the flames, black smoke spewing skyward.

Holly hell! Heidi unhooked her bathing suit top and began to tie off his wrist with a tourniquet. The men began taking off their shirts, attempting to staunch the blood. Brandon finally realized he'd cut off his hand but was unable to form words. His sister's scream was piercing, like a kettle with endless water jiggling on the stove. The shrieks sent the birds in the boughs and Jira fleeing into the cave. Heidi imagined this might be what trumpets ushering the end of the world might sound like.

CHAPTER 6

Marley Vega

MARLEY HAD HIS PULSE ON the island as much as anyone and there was something weird going on. It wasn't just the congregation of zombies boozing it up in Cava after a sleepless night. Or the tourists wandering aimlessly on the resort grounds. Their rhythms had been thrown out of whack, like the tides, like the howler monkeys shrieking alarm in the nearby jungle. This constant state of agitation was unusual. Had the howlers also been unable to sleep? News pundits, scientists and doctors traded barbs on the satellite channels, set now to captions because of the chatter in all corners of Cava. There was no business as usual anymore, in the world or on Devil's Caye.

On Saturdays, Marley traded bottles of whiskey from their stash for fresh fish first thing in the morning. But today the locals hadn't made the customary trip over from D-town. The maids and restaurant staff hadn't made the trek over yet, either. By now, he would have normally slipped out with a free cup of coffee to Enrique, a local artist who crafted sculptures from the flotsam washed up on the beach, along with a promise to send a tourist or two his way. Not today though. Alcohol had called them all on a Saturday to gather in a congregation, liquid spirits a stronger pull than even God.

Mid-afternoon loomed and it was usually dead at the bar. He had an unspoken agreement with Daniela to go over to the resort and help haul the used towels from the poolside over to the laundry when he had downtime at Cava. Daniela would reward him for his efforts with a piece of mango pie, while she ran the industrial-sized washer. She'd always gone out of her way to make himself and Rex feel at home here. She also picked up their laundry once a week in exchange for an open tab at the bar. She never abused this privilege, never sucked down more than her usual Rum and Diet Coke. Daniela was usually a rock, but tonight she was as solid as the cliffs on the northeast coastline of the island, riddled with caves. She was getting drunk enough to reach out and fling an arm around his waist when he stopped by to bus her table.

"Marley, you are a beautiful man hiding in a boy's body."

"Thank you...I think."

"You don't need to be ashamed," she said.

"OK, I'll do my best."

"You've grown so much. I need to tell you something," she said, her voice slurred like a motor that wouldn't turn over. "But before that I need to tell you something else."

Marley was embarrassed without knowing exactly why. He felt the bubbling need surrounding him. Hands jabbed skyward for drinks that would not drown out their fears. He took a long look at the smooth round face of his favorite woman on the island, perhaps the favorite woman in his entire life.

"There's a storm coming," she said, gripping his arm tightly.

"There usually is."

"You're not listening. The tide is high on the north side. D-town will be underwater first storm."

"Jesus," he said. It made sense, though. The south side of the island had reclaimed at least fifty feet of sand at low tide. Tendrils of the reef occasionally poked out above the surf. It made sense that D-town would have the opposite problem. Here was his dirty secret: he headed over to the other side of the island as little as possible. Partially, it was because he didn't have much in common with the fisherman husbands of the maids who worked at Copeland Resort. Partially, he felt uncomfortable with the poverty. Even though he busted his hump at the bar he sensed that everyone knew that he came from money. And would always have money. His summer job was just another role, like the ones he'd perfected in school plays and with his more dramatic friends. His safety net was pretending that he was anyone other than himself.

"Some of the huts are already taking in water," Daniela said.

"What are the D-towners doing about it?"

"Everything they can. That hunk of a SEAL Rick hauled over empty bags to fill with sand. And he's over there helping them build a wall. Everyone is angry and afraid. They feel abandoned and they're not thinking straight."

"No one is," Marley said, but that wasn't true. The tiredness made him feel less anxious than usual, more connected with the world around him.

"Wait until everyone starts to panic," she said.

Her eyes were on Russell Copeland, and she clenched her drink like a policeman would his baton, all business. The resort owner and his ex-wife Maxine huddled around a phone, holding it to their ears, handing it back and forth. Marley slipped out of Daniela's hold and could feel her nails scrape his skin. He wandered over to their table and heard the name *Nan* more than once. They were trying to be reassuring but had to speak loudly to be heard. Cell service was expensive on the caye, and unreliable. It wasn't long before they'd lost the connection and clutched hands, worried about something they could not control.

Did Marley's own father even care about him? There had been no phone call to the bar, no reassurance that his dad was worried about his wellbeing. As for his mother, she was a lost cause, in another country, in another state of mind. Never a factor in his childhood or looming adulthood. It seemed the entire bar was beckoning to him, but Marley didn't care. He was starting to freak the fuck out and couldn't get out of his own head. They could get off their own asses and stumble to the bar to order. He needed a moment to feel the wind on his skin, to gather himself.

He stepped out on the patio and descended the small staircase to the beach. The wind whistled some tune from his childhood. Had it always done that? Like a whistle to call a dog. He shivered involuntarily and marched toward a figure sitting cross-legged on a hill. The act itself confused him. Why did he feel the need to seek company? Why was he heading straight toward a tourist staring at a tablet like it held the secrets of the universe?

The young man did not look up from the screen as he approached, and Marley plopped down next to him. He was your standard hipster white guy with long black hair tied in a ponytail, his long face saved from awkwardness by a beard and the mostly hidden remains of scars from acne. The dude had a tattoo of a surfboard in the hand of a giant. Was it cutting into his bicep or was that slash of red a sunset over the waves?

"I'm getting married tomorrow."

"Congrats, dude," Marley said.

"It's a sham, the whole relationship," he said, flipping his ponytail like the metronome of a clock to some internal rhythm. "My father wants me to be a doctor and my fiancée wants me to be a writer. My mother wants me to be married and I want to walk away and not look back but I'm not Jesus."

"Excuse me?" Marley asked.

"I can't just stroll across the water."

"No shit. I'm Marley."

"Trevor Keith" he said, "I'm a man with two first names and a wife who wants me to take her last name."

When they shook hands, Marley glanced at the screen and he saw Kara, Trevor's naked bride-to-be, playing the role of lunchmeat in a George family sandwich.

"That's messed up," Marley said.

"Would you believe me if I told you that I deserve it?"

"How so?"

"I'm a writer...or a wannabe writer."

"Cool," Marley said, fighting down the urge to say *me too*.

"I've done a few unethical things to make a name for myself, including working at a marina where rich people hang out. This is where I met Kara."

"Maybe she saw something in you?" Marley suggested, surprised by how quickly the two "failed" writers on the island were bonding.

"Just in the image I projected. I wanted to make connections in Hollywood, to convince people that I'm talented. Kara believed my bullshit...at first. Until I made a huge mistake."

Marley rode the pause for a moment and imagined this was how he got

42

Kara so interested in him. "What was it? I'll bite."

"She read my screenplay. On the flight over. I was sleeping and she was bored. I really messed things up."

"What does that matter? You're still getting married, right?"

"Yes, but she thought it sucked."

"Did she say that?"

"She didn't need to. I've lost all my power over her. The spell is broken."

An engine sputtered and the charter boat *Georgeous* roared toward the resort dock. It was going way too fast. Trevor dropped his tablet on the dune and ran toward the dock. Marley paused, momentarily, at the images flashing on screen. The bodies pressed together drew his gaze and it felt like looking at the sun, something beautiful but could leave a mark. By the time he broke out of his stupor all hell was breaking out on the pier. Half the Cava bar had emptied out, it seemed.

On the boat, Brandon George was shaking and moaning on the cockpit chair while Heidi appeared to be applying a bandage to his arm. What looked like blood was everywhere: on the passengers now scrambling onto the dock, on the boat deck, and on the bandage at the end of Brandon's arm. Marley wandered farther down the dock and looked into a Styrofoam container with the handle of machete and a hand waving to him from inside. Gross. Not knowing what to do, Marley picked up the container and carried the cooler back toward Brandon, setting it down at his feet. He wasn't sure if the hand could be saved but it was better than it being forgotten. By now the crowd from the bar had reached the dock to find out what the commotion was, and the parents of the bride and groom were about to tell them when Barbara yelled from the boat. "Is anyone here a fucking doctor?"

The crowd looked at each other, and a few looked away. Trevor saw his fiancé Kara and gave her a wave like a man with a plan. "We don't have any doctors," he said.

"How the hell do you know?"

"It's my wedding and I know everyone here."

"How about at the base?" Barbara shouted, in the direction of Heidi's boyfriend Rick who'd pushed to the front of the crowd.

"No, we have basic medic training, but nothing like you'll need," he said, stepping from the pier and into the boat with no wasted motion. "Good tourniquet, babe."

"Learning through osmosis," Heidi replied, as she struggled to keep Brandon from falling off the side.

"Fuck this then, everyone off. I'm taking my brother to Belize City."

"You need one more person with you. One to watch after your brother and another to steer the boat," Rick said. "Maybe I should do it so I can track down my squad on the mainland."

"She needs someone who can help steer the boat in a pinch," Brandon said, his eyes fluttering open momentarily before shutting again.

Trevor shuffled to the front of the crowd. "I can drive this boat with my eyes closed," he said. "I'll help you get him to shore."

Kara stepped forward out of her parents' embrace and asked, "What about our wedding?"

"I'll be back in the morning to get hitched…if that's OK?" Trevor looked at Barbara, who nodded, and took over looking after Brandon from Heidi so she could leave.

Rick and Heidi got off the boat and Trevor got on. *Was this fool trying to play the hero for a woman?* Marley couldn't tell for sure, but nothing about their situation felt natural. He was confused and knew that it would only get worse.

"I'll get us out of here," Trevor said. "I assume you have the route in your GPS?"

"Yes." Barbara pressed the bandage over her brother's stump with one hand while flexing her fingers in the air with the other. It was like she was making sure her own range of motion had not been impacted by the machete. "Careful you don't go aground. The tide has made all the passages shallower."

Trevor untied his hoodie from his waist and slipped his arms inside, dramatically zipping up and waiting for the inevitable *"don't go's"* from his family and groomsmen. Nothing emanated from Kara, though. She marched to the boat railing and, as though cameras were on her, blew an air kiss. Her bridesmaids, led by her diminutive blonde maid of honor Stacy, huddled around her in a group hug. Maybe there was something to be said for acting as though an audience was always watching. The world had suddenly turned into a reality show with everyone facing drama at unprecedented levels.

CHAPTER 7

Russell Copeland

THAT NIGHT, RUSSELL FELT THE PRESSURE of being a resort owner. When his guests asked him what should be done during the crisis, he did his best to deflect attention. He kept the wedding party focused on the ceremony the next afternoon. He funneled the guests to the poolside cafe and kept out of sight. Normally, he was gregarious and liked to make the rounds, taking on all comers at ping pong or cards of all varieties. He felt like they could see through to the core of his inadequacies. His short blond hair was dotted with gray strands hiding in the forest, the whole cut designed to minimize the bald spots migrating from his forehead backwards. His skinniness was from his smoking habit and not exercise. Even a short walk on the beach, like now, could wind him.

He was doubly hiding from his ex, Maxine. After the groom-to-be Trevor Keith pushed off to Belize City with the Boys George, he took the opportunity to slip away. The allure of drinking was too enticing as the lack of sleep blurred all lines, including his attraction to his former wife. She had been sitting too close to him at Cava and he could feel himself inhabiting a younger version of himself, one with a lascivious appetite for booze, pills, and sex with a buxom redhead. While the wedding party watched the boat disappear in the distance, Daniela slipped off from the periphery and began climbing a sand dune toward the nearest forest path. Russell took the opportunity to follow after her in the hopes of catching up and having a heart to heart. She'd shot him several dirty looks earlier in the bar and he'd deserved it. Even though talking to his daughter had been a priority he shouldn't have let Maxine drive a wedge between them. She should have been by his side instead of getting drunk at another table.

How to make up for it? Well, he could start by telling her how he felt. She was his work-wife and lover. She listened to his bullshit and helped him stay sober. They both had secrets they hadn't revealed. He knew she was keeping things from him but how could he blame her? He was doing the same thing himself. He justified that he was simply giving her room to talk when she was ready even while another part of himself was thankful for not having yet another set of responsibilities to deal with. Christ, it was complicated falling in love as a geezer.

He was huffing and puffing now in earnest, his feet aching in sandals, and dizziness from a lack of food and sleep. She hadn't yet noticed him, and he thought about calling out. The sun hovered just above the tree line, and he followed Daniela into the jungle. This path led to D-town and jutted out to a circuit of spindly paths used as short cuts across the island in all directions. These other trails were less well maintained, a spider-web of interlocking paths. He'd never gone off the beaten path, except once with Daniela to visit the abandoned church hidden away in the middle of the jungle. In a clearing now overgrown with saplings, a bent cross had been barely visible over the foliage that strangled a crumbling stone structure in a nest of green. The church had been devastatingly beautiful, like Daniela, but he'd been too careful to say anything of the sort to her.

His mind wandered to the nexus of trails in his life, the paths not taken, the ones filled with tragedies, large and small. For the first time in weeks, he thought of his father, a man who'd loved the woods and hunting. The old man had chided him for his lack of focus and killer instinct on their wilderness excursions, relegating him to picking berries with his mother. Her only escape from them both was chain smoking and later the cancer and eventual suicide from the pain. His memory of her drifted away like flotsam

46

in one of Pittsburgh's rivers. He'd hated his father for driving them to two divergent paths: one to dying and one to becoming a killer.

"What the hell are you doing?" Daniela called out abruptly. "You're wandering out here like a ghost."

"Yes, a ghost," he said. Russell tried to snap back to his senses. She must have heard him tracking her and popped out from behind a tree to find out who was stalking her. Even though her tone was sharp, she knew him well enough not to grab him and make him shriek from fear.

"Where's your wife?"

"Ex-wife," Russell said. "I want to explain."

"Ok, explain why your wife is staying in your bed."

"I didn't sleep there, Daniela."

"No one is sleeping. That's the point. The world is ending, and you're supposed to be with the people that matter. I thought we mattered. To each other."

Sunlight dappled her skin through the tangle of leaves spread in a canopy above them. She was shrinking away from him; he could feel it. His own source of light was disappearing into the undergrowth. A distant terror felt now so close. He reached over to pull her to his chest, accustomed to the way her small hands burrowed into his chest hair. Her body was stiff, at first, before she took him in her arms, and they swayed. They trembled with the wind.

"We do matter," Russell said. "You and I are a team."

"We'll see. Days like these will push people away from each other. Fear. Anger. Desperation. It's all around us. Even the trees seem scared of us."

This was a strange thought. Even though Daniela wasn't overly religious she was spiritual in the way of all women looking to believe the men in their lives weren't total shits.

"We'll face this together," he promised, even as he could sense some forest spirit stalking him, the shade of his father perhaps, or all hunters who died horrible deaths.

"OK, she said, her eyes brimming with tears. "Come with me to D-town. I need to check on my other family."

Other family? This was a topic she normally avoided: her complicated relationship with her uncle and D-town patriarch Jira Santos, the complicated set of influences on the other side of the island where she'd spent the majority of her life. Even at twenty-five, Daniela was an old soul, a rooted woman with more wisdom than he'd managed to gain in his half-life in purgatory first waiting for his father to die, then afterward when he was unable to get over it.

Daniela's hand tugged him forward and the evening unfolded as though time was not linear but rolling up into itself. They strolled hand-in-hand through the jungle. The shadows loomed around them as did the shrieks of howler monkeys and the squawks of birds oscillating halfway between agitation and alarm, perhaps themselves now unable to dream. The trek took much longer than it should have or else he was lost—in thoughts, in his past, in his helplessness around women, even one he loved.

Eventually, they emerged from the jungle into D-town at dusk. D-town was a misnomer, of course. It was a village, really, home to twenty or so islanders. The beach had its own ramshackle dock for a handful of ancient fishing boats. The village consisted mostly of huts in various stages of disrepair, a convenience store littered with candles of saints and canned goods teetering on the ends of their expiration dates, and a massive circular building nicknamed *Thunderdome* that served as school, church, and community center. The dome was the only structure that had been built with cement. It was far enough from the beach to not be at risk from the rising tides pushing against the sandbags that had been fashioned into a flimsy bulwark against the waves.

They passed Jira Santos, the D-stop owner, the ancient hellcat who'd scrapped with Wolf Granger on the night the moon changed its orbit. In this half-light, he looked spry, many years younger than when Russell had seen him last, two nights before. Perhaps, this malady, this sleeplessness had imbibed him with power and purpose. Jira snorted and made the sign of the devil as they passed. His tattoo of a demon on his shoulder stared at Russell. He could feel the red eyes still watching long after they passed. Daniela gripped his arm. Her relationship with her uncle had shifted over the past few years. Jira had renounced her after she refused to worship in his cult and follow his bizarre brand of Christianity intermingled with local customs. He

48

was dangerous in the way of all zealots who believed that their belief was the only path to salvation.

Russell absently watched the wind whip the water. The sky had clouded over considerably in the past few hours, and he could sense a storm brewing. The whitecaps swelled in the gloaming. Daniela's nails dug into his palms. He snapped out of his reverie and followed her line of sight. Most of the village, the fishermen and their wives who worked at his resort, huddled exhaustedly around a bonfire.

He hadn't learned yet the names of most of the men, even though the island was not large, and he'd seen them coming and going during their workdays. He did see the muscular fisherman Juan and his younger brother John, a diminutive version with barrel chest and bulging biceps, only six inches shorter and fifty pounds lighter. Juan wore a *Genesis* concert T-shirt and John a *Spuds Mackenzie* sleeveless muscle shirt. Each clutched a Budweiser like it was a lifeline. Part of him wondered if they'd gotten their shirts from those left behind by tourists a generation before or if they perused bargain bin sales on eBay. These types of questions were a bridge too far, however. Russell did not feel comfortable on this side of the island. It was clear that he was an interloper, an outsider, a yet-to-be-trusted employer to many of them.

"I'm famished," he whispered, not knowing what else to say. His stomach was a knot that momentarily made him forget about his uneasiness.

"Come with me," she said. "I've got you covered."

Daniela waved to the onlookers gathered around the crackling flames and a few hands rose in the smoke to greet her. Russell nodded and tried to appear nonchalant. Inside, he was freaking out and his legs were leaden. Daniela led him up the beach past several dunes to a shack located on a mound of grass that separated the sand from their communal gardens. Russell had seen the crops once before, on his first and only visit to D-town. Small plots of vegetables and melons were separated by tiny fences, each family with their own plot.

Daniela knocked lightly on the outside of the door and marched inside without waiting for a response. Lilian, one of his maids, and her husband Enrique were picking at plates filled with snapper, beans, and rice. They were tired and appeared to have been fighting. Enrique smiled but his face was streaked with dirt and possibly tears. Lilian rose from the table and rushed over to hug Daniela. "Join us for dinner. Both of you. There's always room for family."

"We're cousins," Daniela explained. "Jira's her father."

"I asked Dani not to tell you so I wouldn't get special treatment," Lilian said. She was short and compact like her cousin, both in their mid-twenties with an air of self-reliance. There was something else, too, that bubbled up— an uneasiness in her quick brown eyes that flashed around the room. He'd seen it in her demeanor at the resort. She was either not quite present or all-too present, always looking for something out of place to be fixed or cleaned. It made her good at her job and a looming presence. What would it be like to live with such a woman?

"Russell, please let us get you a plate," Enrique said. "I have another painting to show you that I think you'll like."

"This is hardly the time to try to sell him something." Lilian stepped in front of Enrique before he could get to the stove.

"I'm proud of my art. Unlike some people here."

Lilian rolled her eyes and snorted. "I'm proud of keeping a roof over our heads."

"Jesus, not this again. I just wanted my friend's opinion."

"Enrique, I'd love to see what you're working on," Russell said.

The tension was deflated, for the moment. Daniela joined her cousin in the open kitchen, while Enrique led him to an alcove across from their bedroom, separated from the rest of their domicile by a curtain of beads. The clatter of plates, cutlery, and utensils scraping made Russell salivate in hunger. He followed Enrique into a cozy nook with almost no walking space between stereo, hammock, and a table cluttered with acrylics and brushes, with the window cracked to help with the smell of paint in close quarters. On a plywood easel, he saw the same haunted man who hung in the reception area of his resort. This time the model was clothed in camouflage gear and leaned against a tree, holding a rifle and staring angrily at a songbird in the branches. The likeness to his father was striking. Jesus, this must have been why he'd been drawn to the painting he'd bought in the first place.

"This is intense," Russell said. "I feel sick."

"It's your predecessor, Quinn. He spent a lot of time here in D-town."

"He looks like a real son of a bitch," Russell said, but he wasn't quite able to mask the terror rising inside of him. Rumor had it that Quinn had gone mad after the devastation of the hurricane and went bankrupt trying to rebuild it into a high-end eco-tourist destination. He'd never met the man, only traded in innuendos with his lawyer as they negotiated the purchase of the land (and naming rights to the caye).

"He is almost as much of a devil as Jira. The two of them fought for the hearts and minds of D-town, but Quinn lost when the paychecks stopped. The bastard wandered around the island like a spirit before finally heading off in a boat to find a new island to call his own. It was a mad plan by a madman. Everyone was happy to see him go, though."

"Except you. He seems like he was your favorite subject."

Enrique smiled. "Him and Jira both. But Lilian gets mad at me whenever I paint her uncle."

He looked at Lilian and Daniela carrying two plates over to the table. They were in their twenties but were more responsible than he'd been at that age. They were confident women with seemingly no pressure to become mothers. Not everyone was like him, he realized, dragged into parenthood only because it seemed like it was expected of him by everyone. His secret was that he regretted fatherhood. Something he wasn't supposed to admit, even to himself.

They sat together at dinner and discussed the day's events, the wobbling moon and lost hand, the news pundits and unclear prognosis, and the lopsided tides. After a few more beers, even the strange appearance of Russell's first wife Maxine was fair game. Russell shared a few stories about how she'd cheated on him with his best friend, not for any purpose other than to break his heart and spirit. Daniela told him that he would have worse to deal with if he were to ever treat her poorly. Russell found himself laughing when he confided to his drinking companions that he'd broken his sobriety, having somehow forgotten that he was an addict. The world was not ending as much as it was spinning backwards.

Daniela led him to a hammock next to the artist's easel and they settled in for some down time. Even if sleep was not possible, they both needed to unplug. Russell made sure that his head on her chest was angled so that he faced toward the window instead of staring at his father's creepy doppelganger on the canvas. They heard what sounded like lovemaking nearby, through the beaded curtain in the young couple's bedroom. Daniela's hand did not stray below his chest.

For hours they talked, and it turned into babbling, on both their parts. For the first time she mentioned her father, a politician in Belize City who she almost never saw and who'd provided an occasional check that she'd being stashing away until she had enough to move away from Devil's Caye, from the only home she'd ever known. She told him that he should sell the resort and go with her, that the land here was cursed, for the whites and browns, for the storms and tragedies that passed from one side of the island to the other, from one generation to the next. At some point, the storm hit, and the couple held each other, the hut rocking from the winds that wailed like the dead, water dripping from the beams like the drooling mouth of God.

"My father was a son of a bitch, too," he repeated like a mantra when it became clear that they would not be able to hear each other over the thunder and rain. When the storm reached its crescendo, he heard footsteps rushing outside, and the alarmed voices of Lilian and Enrique. Finally, the window and door stopped clacking and the rain stopped plopping on the wood. The silence was strangely compelling. They disentangled themselves from the hammock and each other, out into the first light of a new day.

It was madness. The beach had disappeared, and the tide had risen to within a few feet of the hut. The water was starting to recede, but the homes in the rest of the village had vanished. Off the face of the earth. No, that wasn't quite right. Several jagged roofs jutted up just above the waterline. The entire row of huts had been swallowed by the ocean, by the swollen tide confused by the winds and a displaced moon.

"C'mon, Russell, let's see if we can help," Daniela said, her voice trembling.

"We're all screwed," he said, but gripped her hand and raced with his girlfriend close to the tree line, dodging the rivulets of ocean water clawing almost to the jungle.

"We're used to this. To hurricanes. To tragedy. The moon will not be the end of us," Daniela promised.

Russell was not so sure. Two days without sleep had turned him into a man falling back into old habits, sweating through every interaction, and scared of his phantoms looming around him. Ghosts lived in this realm without sleep. And they would grow in their powers.

"Not today," Russell admitted, unable to shake the feeling he was being watched.

"Jesus, why did this happen to us? Why not the other side of the island?"

"Life isn't fair," Russell said.

"No, it never is. You rich guys come here to make a fortune, but the island gets its revenge. Every time."

"What are you talking about?" Russell asked.

"Devil's Caye always gets its flesh and blood. You're a marked man."

"I knew the risks when I bought the place."

"You don't know anything."

He paused. This sounded like something Maxine might say to him. Perhaps, his women problems were from his own lack of convictions.

"I know I care about you," he finally spat out.

"We should grab a boat and leave. Now," Daniela insisted.

"You're tired. None of us are thinking straight."

They trudged up a rise to a clearing next to the main path to the resort. Here they took in the remains of D-town. Only two buildings had escaped the flooding—the D-stop, with padlocked door and shuttered windows, and the Thunderdome brimming with lights and voices crackling with energy. All of D-town, apparently, was inside.

"This island is ours. And we need to take back what's ours," Jira's voice boomed from the walls as though amplified, his preacher's insistence imbuing the ad-hoc sermon with power and emotion. The voices of the villagers hooted angrily. It dawned on Russell that he was not safe here, would never be safe here. He needed to escape but he wasn't fast enough to ever run from the danger he posed to himself.

One of the fishermen pushed Daniela away from him and his body lurched into motion. He remembered the sting of branches on his face and cries, perhaps from the monkeys or else Daniela. He rushed headlong through the forest, scared of everyone and everything. His bare feet were bleeding and his legs cramped from exhaustion, from too little water. After what seemed an eternity, he found himself outside the front door of his cabana and looked out at the sunrise setting the ocean on fire. He was in hell. No, perhaps in purgatory. He pushed the door and it creaked open. Before he could step inside, he was met with a fist to the gut.

"Asshole, you deserve that and a whole lot more," Owen Frank said.

Russell had fallen on his ass on the sandy walkway and took in reality from a dwarf's perspective. The naval officer zipped his trousers and buckled his pants, looking at him like he was a piece of trash. What the hell?

Maxine was behind Owen, in one of the resort robes, with her carry-on bag draped over her shoulder. She blew him a kiss and said, "The Commander took care of my needs all night and convinced me that I should be with him where it's safe with the SEALs."

"She deserves more than a junkie," Owen said and shouldered him out of the way.

"Honey, we'll all do what we need to survive," Maxine said. "I don't trust you. Our daughter needs me to live."

He watched Maxine grab Owen's hand and wander down the beach. From behind, they looked as normal as any couple at the resort.

"Enjoy your little native whore," Owen called out.

Daniela? He'd abandoned her. He was truly lost, but not alone. In the shadows of the tree, he could sense his father watching over him.

CHAPTER 8

Heidi Radar

JESUS, HEIDI WOULDN'T HAVE THOUGHT it was possible until today—there was such a thing as too much sex, too much exercise, too much sweat. Too much time on your hands. Heidi and Rick had both hit the wall in their strategies for managing through their lack of sleep. With the internet down (temporarily they hoped), they were now unable to check in on the latest news on the global search for an insomnia cure. Between their horizontal workouts, Rick obsessed about his squad and shared how he felt responsible for them. It wasn't the first time he'd lost men. He got separated from his squad on a SEAL mission somewhere in Afghanistan and he never discovered what had happened to them. They haunted his dreams, and because there were no longer dreams, his waking hours.

The moon's new orbit had done more than turn the tide topsy-turvy. It had transformed humanity into zombies just before the hunger took hold. The last reports before their wi-fi stopped working detailed how many governments were now declaring martial law. Airline travel had been banned in the U.S. after the first commercial liner crashed in the Pacific. Scientists were taking volunteers by the thousands for experimental treatments, but so far, no breakthroughs. At least, none reported.

The online search "how long can you live without sleep" had started beating all other queries except for perhaps "suicide." The niceties and rules for human interactions were now strained. The sleep-crazed inhabitants of the planet were hurtling toward an anarchic flashpoint. Crime rates ballooned. More and more government employees weren't showing up for work. The grid that sustained their lives was in danger. Everything and everyone were boiling to a flashpoint.

After watching two movies from the '80s on VHS during the thunderstorms, they ended up wresting in bed like brother and sister. She started pinching him and he eventually shoved a pillow in her face, arm outstretched, to keep her fingernails at bay.

Black spots danced in her eyes and fire filled her from head to toe. She screamed at him incoherently, angrily, and slugged him in the shoulder. He yelped and looked betrayed. Her flesh crawled and her instincts were fight or flight. Without thinking, she raced barefoot through the empty corridors straight out to the naval docks. Sunrise stained the ocean with blood and even her dolphins were agitated. She ignored them, ignored the pain in her knuckles, ignored the need to change into her swimsuit.

Heidi hurried past the boats and wondered if the other SEALs would ever return to their island base, or if anything would ever be the same. Even the ocean smelled different post-rain, with shifting winds cradling the scent of electricity and the whispers of an earth looking to churn over and start anew. She stepped off the dock and the jolt of water brought her back to herself. Her shortness of breath and panic faded away, and her body moved with a mind of its own. Swimming helped her to regulate the oxygen to her lungs and dampen her emotions spiraling out of control. The whimpers of the dolphins behind her brought her back to a girl sitting in her closet nestled in blankets, her sleeping hidey-hole growing up.

Breathe from alternate sides, every four strokes, she thought to herself, and the rhythm took her even further into her past. She remembered an angry man straddling her in bed, telling her to be quiet, holding a pillow over her mouth to stifle her crying. She felt the terror of suffocation, of never breathing again, of leaving her body to try to escape the monster over her. *No daddy*, she said, and choked momentarily. She looked up and coughed, spitting out ocean water and cursing her carelessness, scared of what she'd dredged up from childhood. Her father Marcos had only lived with them until she was eight, before her mother kicked him out. Supposedly for infidelity. Her memories of their days as a nuclear family were spotty at best, and now she understood why. Infidelity? That was a pretty bow to tie around his actions. *Bastard*.

She began treading water and slowly spun in a 360, trying to make sense of her own visions. The shore was nearly a mile away. From this vantage point she should be able to see D-town, but the rooftops of the huts were no longer visible. It was as though the village had been wiped from the earth. Perhaps this was a trick of the shifting shoreline and the tidal abnormalities from the moon strike? Her momentum carried her out toward the open ocean, and that's when she saw the orange life vest and the man floating with burns on his face and chest. It was Trevor Keith, the groomsman returning for his wedding day, unconscious, perhaps dead. Against all decorum or decency, Heidi found herself laughing and unable to stop as the sun edged up over the water. Yes, it was just another day in paradise.

She had trained as a lifeguard working at a summer camp for rich kids in Pasadena, and her body seemed to know what to do, even as she couldn't stop her body from convulsing in laughter, then tears. She was losing her shit bigtime, but the rhythm of the backstroke helped. She was exhausted but invigorated, as though the effort to save a life had allowed her to tap into a hidden reservoir of strength.

A pair of strong hands helped her lift Trevor from the water. Rick scooped the unconscious man into his arms, and she scraped her belly pulling herself up onto the dock. The pain was welcomed. Everything now was some tier of pain. She wanted to explain her feelings but didn't understand them herself. He shook his head when she stammered. *They had bigger fish to fry*, one of his favorite expressions. Dripping wet, she followed Rick and his cargo past the classrooms to the infirmary, a small room jutting out from the smaller of two kitchens in the refurbished mansion.

While she stripped Trevor's clothes and began dabbing lotion on his burns, Rick unlocked the drug cabinet. "Shock" was the only word he spoke, and Heidi didn't know whether that referred to her hasty departure or to

Trevor's condition. Clint Jenkins, stalker that he was, spotted them when he strolled into the adjacent kitchen to drink milk directly from the carton. The very last of their fresh supply. Asshat. The dude didn't even bother closing the refrigerator door or put away the milk. That's when the waft of something dying made its way to the infirmary. The stench couldn't be from the fridge, or could it? Jesus, she was losing it. Clint was no longer it the kitchen. He must have hightailed it up to the Commander's office because it wasn't long before EVERYONE at the base was milling around the unconscious man oozing now from the burns on his face, chest, and neck.

"This man is not our problem and shouldn't even be here," a red-headed woman said, her arm resting on Owen's bicep.

"No offense, but who the hell's this?" Heidi asked.

"Someone looking out for us," the red-headed woman shot back.

"Us?" Rick asked, his thick right eyebrow raised in a gesture that Heidi had always found endearing. "First of all, this is a naval facility. Second of all, this man is in no position to move."

"I'm Maxine, a guest of your Commander's."

Heidi ignored the stranger and focused her attention on Owen Frank, instead. She'd seen this type of bullshit go on when she worked at strip clubs. One of the dancers would suck up to the owner, and before you knew it you were taking orders from her. Landry rolled up the sleeves on his white dress shirt and helped Heidi bandage some of the oozing sores from the burns. He wasn't squeamish and she wondered if he'd had first-aid training. Their resident Englishman was a mystery shrouded in a pinstripe blue vest and suit pants, and he hadn't been forthcoming with any of them.

"Dude has a concussion," Clint said. "I've had a couple before."

"Of course, you have," Heidi said. "From the woman beating you senseless after you creep them out."

She was surprised at her tone, at the laughter from Landry, from her concern that Trevor was only the first of many victims this insomnia would claim.

"We need to wake him up so we can find out what happened to him and the islanders he was traveling with," Owen said.

"Islanders?" Heidi asked. "We're all in this together."

"No, we aren't, honey. This is a U.S. facility, and you can't be too careful," Maxine said.

"Don't honey me," Heidi said. "Why does someone's girlfriend get a voice in what goes on around here?"

"We could say the same thing about you," Clint said with a slurp of self-satisfaction.

"I…WAS…INVITED…HERE!" Heidi annunciated each word with clenched fists and imagined pummeling Clint within an inch of his life.

"I need everyone to calm the fuck down," the Commander said. "Rick, hand me the adrenaline."

"I'd advise against it," Heidi said. "He needs rest, not to relive his trauma."

The Commander ignored her and took the syringe from Rick. He jammed the needle into Trevor's chest like she'd once seen in *Pulp Fiction*. The movie got that part right. Trevor jerked up into a sitting position and said "Pirates" before seeing the needle plunged into the hilt. His eyes fluttered and Heidi withdrew it from his chest.

"It was a bunch of fucking pirates," Trevor continued, and shared with them, at a breakneck pace, how their fishing boat had been rammed and its other passengers lost at sea.

It wasn't long before the mania turned into exhaustion, and Trevor slumped back onto the table, muttering to himself as though reliving the incident over and over again. It was hard to separate what was exhaustion and mania from lack of sleep, or whether he was concussed from the explosion that destroyed the boat. Trevor, himself, told them how to bandage his burns. Apparently, the guy had been pre-med or a writer. Hard to tell from the jumble of words tumbling out of his mouth

Heidi was too unsettled to stay and volunteered to share the news about what happened with Trevor's fiancée and the rest of the wedding party at the resort.

"Only two people can come visit him," Maxine ordered. "We need to keep order."

"What the hell? Owen, are you going to let her boss me around?" Heidi asked.

"That's Commander to you and, yes, that's a fine idea. We don't want this place overrun with riffraff. You can round up two civilians to come and take him back."

"Commander, we shouldn't move him for at least a day," Rick said, as though trying to stave off the string of expletives forming on Heidi's lips.

"Fine, then bring back two visitors. And no funny business," Owen said, leading Maxine to the kitchen where he sat, and she started making him oatmeal for breakfast.

Rick rubbed Heidi's shoulder and she forced herself to smile even if she irrationally felt like breaking his fingers. Why did she have so much rage? It went beyond the hopelessness she felt, and that they all must be feeling. She nodded good-bye to Landry and ignored Clint sitting with a smirk on his face on a stool in the corner of the makeshift infirmary.

She felt the obnoxious trainee's eyes on her and revulsion shimmied through her body. What an asshole. Her anger only deepened when she spotted Maxine, the stranger in their midst, leaning suggestively against the counter waiting for water to boil, arms crossed beneath her breasts. Heidi couldn't stop herself from shooting Maxine the bird behind Owen's back on her way out the door. The redhead did the worst thing possible. She smiled like the cat that ate the canary that had devoured the world.

Heidi's anger drove her racing down the beach. She sprinted from the compound, from the panic that threatened to overtake her, from her shadow snapping at her feet along the beach. She imagined that she was a djinn, a sand demon who could cast her enemies aside and even rip the flesh off bones. Enemies, did she have enemies? The men in her life were always candidates. Her father. Owen Frank. Even Rick was suspect. They all smothered you one way or another. Energy spent, she found the winds dying down around her and collapsed on a dune overlooking a gigantic tent that had been erected for the wedding in a clearing next to the docks.

Kara was dancing for an invisible audience in her wedding dress, slicing the air with the whirling, lacy, and almost see-through wings of a pale, land-bound butterfly. The parents of the bride and groom, from Heidi's nightmare boat trip, were also there. Yesterday. Was it just yesterday? The bride's parents were sitting at a table smoking cigarettes. The grooms' parents stood

60

at the podium with vacant eyes, staring out over the water. They were still preparing for the wedding of the injured man back at the base, a blabbering lunatic with a fricasseed face and arms. Yes. That's why she was here. The bridesmaids, in blue chiffon backless dresses, were chasing each other along the beach. They flapped around in a drunken stupor as many of them had been since the moon had spun like a top out of control.

Heidi stood and raced down the dune into the wedding interrupted. It was then she noticed the resort owner, Russell Copeland, clutching the bible, the justice of the peace. Everyone stopped what they were doing, and she felt eyes stabbing at her from every direction.

"Trevor is hurt. Badly. His boat blew up and he's unable to move or I'm sure he'd make it to his wedding," Heidi said.

"Bad things happen when you're around," Liza Keith said. Trevor's mother took a couple of steps toward Heidi with fists clenched before dropping to her knees.

Heidi couldn't argue with this assessment, even though most of the bad things seemed to happen to her. Russell Copeland helped the mother of the injured man to her feet and started leading her back toward the resort.

"I can't even be the center of attention on my own wedding day," Kara muttered, loud enough to be heard by everyone in the congregation. For some reason, her father, Wolf Granger, clapped his hands once and went back to drinking what appeared to be a mimosa.

"What the hell are we waiting for?" Simon Keith asked, his chest heaving. His hand gripped a flower arrangement so hard that the petals loosened and drifted away along the sands, joining the frolicking bridesmaids. Heidi couldn't believe how less than three days had transformed a professorial looking gentleman into a raggedy version of Colonel Sanders. His facial hair had turned snow white, adding ten years to a man aging seemingly by the second.

"Take me to my son."

One thing that Heidi appreciated was that she hadn't needed to explain the need for only two of them to accompany her back. Simon and Kara trailed behind her wordlessly as they passed by Cava Bar. Too many people flittered inside and outside, far too drunk, many of them pushing the boundaries of alcohol poisoning. A seagull flew into the side of the building and slid to the ground among empty beer bottles, unnoticed to anyone other than herself. She'd seen one of the other dancers do this once at Club Paradise, missing the door jamb by several feet and collapsing lifeless, doll-like to the ground. She couldn't help but feel the impending explosion in the bar. People would continue to lose their grasp on reality once it sunk in that they were all doomed, that madness eventually loomed.

She thought about her mother, hopeless and lost in the Valley, the city of angels filled with devils, her father in Rio watching the hillside favelas pour down into the swank parts of the city, the inevitable fires sending smoke into the air that they would all read for omens. The religious would find some succor in the rapture. Guns would come out of their safes. The senseless violence would take hold as people's nightmares and realities became one and the same. Her thoughts fogged the path ahead, and she was shocked to discover herself inside the SEAL base, sitting at the kitchen table. Kara and Trevor's dad slipped into the infirmary. She could hear their voices. There was rapid-fire dialogue between son, father, and fiancée. Time had jumped or had she just been so lost in her own thoughts she had not tracked how they'd made their way inside. Across from her, Clint Jenkins watched from the same stool he'd been perched on earlier. Must be guard duty. Behind the door out of sight she heard Kara call out loudly, "You don't deserve me."

The rest of their dialogue was only partially audible, but Heidi thought she could hear, "Every bride deserves to be adored on her wedding day. Maybe you should watch your father do what you couldn't."

She heard two no's from father and son, then only from the son, who broke down weeping inconsolably.

"Do it Simon," Kara cried out. "I want him to remember this."

"You're a monster," Simon said. "We're all monsters."

Heidi got up unsteadily to her feet. She wanted to run away, to leave the sickness behind but they were all trapped in a hell of their own making.

CHAPTER 9

Marley Vega

MARLEY'S SPIDEY-SENSE WAS TINGLING. Things had started going very wrong at the Cava bar when the satellite TV went down in the early afternoon. The news programs had alternated between escalating violence and a lack of substantive progress from scientists. Recent efforts had focused on the six astronauts from the US and Russia up in the space station, and their ability to sleep (and dream). Apparently Zero G simulators hadn't solved the problem, or at least that was the official story. Then a conspiracy theory grew hold that these simulators worked and were now being used by the powerful and ultra-rich. Strange hybrids of militia and conspiracy theorists banded together to try to take over any installation that might have such technology. So far, none of this posed any good news for the islanders. There was either no cure, yet, or a cure only for the very well-connected that was being kept hush hush.

If things were grim, they grew even worse once the satellite lost its feed. Internet had stopped working earlier, and getting a phone call through to anywhere was like winning the lottery. Marley hadn't yet been able to get through to his own parents, though he'd only tried his mother once. He'd lost count the number of times he'd hit 1 on his phone to speed-dial his father.

Radio, of all things, was back in the mix. The bar broadcast a station that went by the handle of Reef Radio. They played enough island music to help settle the vibe down, with occasional reports on *Moonsami*, their homespun nickname for the cataclysm. With no TV to focus their collective attention, Marley could sense more tension between the groups inside of Cava: tourists, locals, military. Each now camped in a different section of the bar, with even less mingling as the day wore on. Some debated going to the mainland for help, but these folks were in the minority. Most everyone agreed they were probably better off on an isolated caye than in a more populated area. People in large groups were more dangerous than people in small groups was the general consensus.

"I think everyone is worried about the grid. It's failing," Marley told his grandfather on one of his trips back from bussing tables. He rinsed and washed glasses at a breakneck pace and wondered how long they could both work at peak capacity.

"It's people. They're the ones that are failing," Rex replied.

"What happens if it's the electricity next?" Marley asked. "We're digging into our freezers since our supply boat is MIA."

"We can fish and hunt and climb trees for fruit," Rex said. "Like when I was a boy."

"No one's thinking clearly. People are losing their shit."

"No swearing," Rex admonished, sidling over behind the bar to dry and replace glasses in the cabinet next to the quickly diminishing beer kegs.

"Have you thought about closing down the place?" Marley asked.

"It will get worse, much worse, if we shut the doors."

"How do you figure?"

"This is a water hole, a sanctuary. It's just like with animals out in the wild. They come here to get their needs met and don't attack each other," Rex said.

"That's been true. So far. Without news, without hope, they'll tear each other apart."

"No need to be dramatic," Rex said.

Marley tried not to let this get to him. Grandpapi knew that he was an actor, and it was hard to read what was teasing with his dry sense of humor.

Some of the tourists were in a piss-poor mood. Russell Copeland had set up camp at the bar. Marley poured a shot of rum and the resort owner stared into the brown liquid like it might contain the secret to everlasting life. The would-be wedding party, minus the bride and her father, had relocated to the terrace. Normally, Rex didn't open the enclosed outside space as it was adjacent to their small apartment. He and his grandson had two small bedrooms overlooking the ocean, with a kitchen attached to the adjoining patio between them. The tables outside their home were pregnant with activity. It seemed like the entire island was at Cava, invading their lives.

Everyone had stopped bothering to keep track of time. Day turned to night with little fanfare. Marley hated how people seemed to get crazier in the darkness, with the scarred moon glaring down at them. Several of the guests had already drunk their way to unconsciousness. Perhaps some of these idiots had hoped that it would provide them with sleep. Forced REM. This theory had been blown out of the water yesterday both on TV and with several near-death cases of alcohol poisoning. He had worked with Russell to carry the near comatose drunks over to a corner of the resort's poolside café that Marley had renamed *The Drunk Tank*. He was beyond exhausted as each trip was nearly the length of a soccer field. He'd had to assist a half dozen of the tourists to stumble over there already today, and he was starting to lose it. Maybe servicing the island's unquenchable need for libations had helped him not dwell on what was now obvious: they were all on the path to madness.

Unlike Rex, the foundations that formed his personality were starting to shake. His boisterous façade was there to deflect his doubts about his own strength as a person. He feared many things: critics, bullies, and animals. The first was caused by his own fears that he wasn't talented. The second was for the fact he was a young gay man in Central America, a status that was fraught with peril, even if you came from a family with wealth and influence. The third was rooted in how animals with fangs and claws racked him into a paralyzing fear.

He knew its genesis, of course, but not its cure. His father Gibraltar, before bodyguards, had kept Rottweilers at their house for security. For Marley they were pets. Sometimes they felt more like siblings, and he was the black sheep. His father had raised two brothers from puppies, named them *Death* and *Devil,* and trained them to live up to their names. Both dogs were actually sweet and playful, and they were Marley's best friends when his father kept moving him around from school to school. One summer break when he was twelve, he'd made the mistake of leaning down to pet Devil when he was chomping at his food bowl. Something primal took hold, some instinct to protect food at all costs.

Marley didn't hear the growl, just felt the snap of the fangs and his limp body falling back against the refrigerator. He didn't feel pain, not instantly, but their maid Frida screamed, and he followed suit after seeing the blood spatter on the floor, on his hands, soaking his T-shirt. Fifty stitches later, on his face alongside his right eye, he was called into his father's study and berated for his stupidity. "Now I'll have to kill the dogs," Gibraltar said. Marley begged him not to but later, while he was still in the hospital, was told that it had been done. He was responsible for his own scars and his loneliness at home turned into a hole with no bottom, no light, no ladder. From then on, he would never again reach down to pet a dog, or even a cat. He mistrusted the world of creatures, more so than even that of men.

This fear did not go away over time. Even here, on an island that Americans spent an arm and a leg to visit, he was always on guard. He felt as though the birds, lizards and especially the monkeys had designs on hurting him. Creatures could not be trusted, whether wild or domestic. Humans were their enemy. They must be wising up to the fact that homo sapiens was making the entire planet uninhabitable. There would eventually be hell to pay from all the fish, fowl and beasts of the field.

This worldview made any trek alongside the forest seem like a danger-filled safari. The howler monkeys had lost their damned minds from lack of sleep. As he neared the resort, he was deafened by the hooting and hollering of a tribe of them baying for blood as a large alpha male chased a smaller monkey through the branches above his head. Survival of the fittest. No longer building families but staking territory. A reversal of evolution. Yes, they were all devolving without sleep. Somehow, this moon crash was homing them in on the most primitive portions of their brains.

He would not succumb to his fears. He was a trained actor. The monkeys had no damn idea that he was scared. He pretended that he was his father, lord of all that he surveyed, and marched back toward Cava. It made him feel better to pretend until he thought too long about it. Perhaps there was no core in the center of him solid enough to keep him from drifting away. Even his metaphors felt like they weren't quite hanging together.

He couldn't help but notice how the bride crested a dune and stomped toward Cava across the sand in bare feet, triumphant in her own way. With makeup smeared across her face like war paint, she carried herself like she'd married the world instead of her fiancée apparently now laid up in the SEAL base infirmary. Simon, the groom's father, trailed behind her, deep in thought. Marley had seen grief before in his short life, but this was something else. Despair. Yes. Simon's eyes let out no light like two absent moons.

Marley didn't watch where he was going and nearly tripped over a chair where Enrique had set up shop. Their local artist leaned over his pad, sketching a scene inside the bar with manic strokes of a charcoal nub pinched between thumb and forefinger. The color palette was strange, crimson mixed with the gray. What the hell? Enrique's fingers were soaked in blood, either from a cut or from gripping the charcoal too fervently. The effect was like looking through blood-colored glasses. Perhaps this was how the world appeared now to Enrique, who mixed his blood into his art. For the first time, Marley's tiredness seemed too heavy a burden and he almost toppled over. The sketch made him think about the people inside the bar as the animals they were.

Several shouts from inside Cava made him snap to attention. Enrique didn't even look up as Marley sprinted around him, up the steps, and through the side door. Clint Jenkins, the lone naval trainee who hadn't been cleared to go on shore leave, was cupping his nose and cursing. Blood dripped down his knuckles and onto his white T-shirt. Standing over the trainee was Simon Keith. In the bar's fluorescent glow, Marley noticed the same acne scars pitted on the man's cheekbones as he'd seen on his son Trevor's. Was it scarring that truly tied a family together? If that were the case, his father would need to get his own jagged lines on his cheekbone to bring them closer together.

"I hate the army," Simon yelled at the SEAL with a flushed face, hands clenched into fists. The sunburn in the bald spot on Simon's head glowed bright red in the bar lights.

"We're the navy, you pervert. I saw that you wanted to give it to the bride in front of your own son," Clint said.

"You shut up!" Simon yelled and reared back to kick him. Clint easily dodged the salvo and snatched the man's bare foot. He stood up quickly and sent Simon back into the bridesmaids' table, spilling a pitcher of beer. The remaining bridesmaids scurried to their feet to keep from getting wet and jostled nearby tables.

Simon slapped the nearest bridesmaid across the face and yelled, "Someone please put me out of my misery."

Rick Coslow, the naval demolitions trainer, swooped in out of nowhere like a damned action movie hero. That big dude punched Simon's diaphragm and the fight and air went out of the old man. As the latter straightened up the SEAL grabbed him under the shoulders, partly to keep him upright and partly to try to keep the melee from spreading.

"Is it true that you had sex with the woman our son was supposed to marry?" Liza Keith, the groom's mother, asked. She was the only one who hadn't moved from her seat at the table.

Kara had circled to a spot in front of the television. "Women shouldn't shame other women," she said, staring at the mother of her fiancé with spite and disappointment. "The thing you need to know is that your son couldn't do it and your husband wanted to."

"Now, now," said Wolf Granger, the director stepping into frame in front of his daughter and into the drama's spotlight. "Let's let cooler heads prevail. Anything happening during this period of sleeplessness doesn't count. None of us are ourselves."

"Fuck you," yelled someone from the crowd and a beer glass went flying at Wolf's head. He barely dodged the missile, but it caught his daughter in the head. She went down in a heap.

Wordlessly, the bar erupted in a brawl, an old-fashioned bare-knuckled affair. Two of the fishermen lifted their table and tossed it at the tourists. Clint got up in time to catch the resort owner with a blow in the back of the neck as he led Simon out the front door. In return someone lobbed a chair at

Clint, and it hit his back, to sound of breaking. The chair fell in pieces and Clint clutched his back as though it, too, was broken. Marley kept his head down as shards of broken glass flew everywhere. It was then he heard Rex roar, "Everyone get out!" The cricket bat was in his hands, and he stepped out into the melee, swinging the bat forcefully from side to side.

Marley knew he should wade in behind his Grandpapi to protect his back, but it was all too much for him to bear. He slipped behind the bar for protection, but one of the groom's friends was climbing up to grab a bottle of top-shelf whiskey and at that moment a pair of hands pulled at the man's feet and the crash was epic. Marley bolted into the basement, his refuge from work. At first, he hid behind a couple of boxes of beer but soon heard footsteps descending and rushed into the open supply cage. He closed it from the inside, locking it. The key was around his neck, under his shirt.

The figure approached slowly, and tears filled Marley's eyes. For some reason, he remembered coming across Frida in their wine cellar as she shared the news she'd been fired. She sobbed and ran her red fingernails across his bandages. She had been there when his mother had not, had been a surrogate mother just like the dogs had been surrogate siblings. And in one fell swoop, they were all gone. There would be a cavalcade of hired help after her, but no one who made him feel like he wasn't a freak.

"You're an abomination," a voice purred from the shadows. Jira stepped toward him, his right hand on the blade of a hunting knife already red with blood.

"Fuck off, you god-damn creep," Marley said.

"Using the Lord's name in vain is a sin, but your whole life is a sin."

"Rex!" Marley cried out but the sound that tumbled from his lips was barely more than a whisper.

"Ever notice how a knife looks like a cross?"

Jira, with mad energy, lunged and the knife slid through the mesh of the cage. The blade stopped just short of his chest. Marley brought his hands up to protect his face and stumbled backwards into a box of canned goods. The blade darted in, first from the front, then the sides, as Jira tried to rend him with more wounds, more scars.

"Your salvation will come. Don't you worry."

Marley childishly placed his hands over his eyes and imagined being swept away to a far better place. The noises grew louder for a time then receded. The knife slid along the bars and a voice whispered, "God can hear your prayers because I am God." He shut his eyes tighter and cupped his hands over his ears.

He remembered one of his recurring dreams. His mother, abroad in Europe for most of the year, visited him while he slept. She would help him sort out his homework, navigate how to avoid teasing in the classroom, and show him the proper way to kiss. He was never aroused by this. It seemed natural, that somehow, she loved him here on another plane of reality. Was his mother in Paris thinking about him as her own sanity spooled away?

The smell of smoke brought him to his senses, the crackle of alcohol in flames. Marley jumped to his feet in time to see the basement cage swing open with Rex's own key dangling from it. His grandfather gestured to him, arms outstretched. Yes, Marley was being rescued. There was something wrong, though. Rex's eyes watered and he bent over in pain. He rushed to his grandfather's side but was waved off. The family patriarch rasped, "follow me," and choked on the thickening plumes. Cava, their bar and home, was on fire.

He followed his coughing grandfather up the steps and out the back door. Bodies, bruised and bloodied, lounged on the beach. The divisions had disappeared momentarily. Tourists, islanders, and sailors co-mingled the way they had the first evening when the moon had gotten a black eye. They all watched the bonfire of the bar, sparks and flames crackling skyward. The puffy faces were now sedate, as though all they needed were marshmallows and someone playing guitar to feel all was right with the world. Jira, that bastard, had disappeared. Rex held his ribs with one hand, as though cramping, and tossed the other arm around Marley, the only hug he could ever remember getting from his tough-as-nails grandfather. It had the desired effect. Marley's breaths elongated and his forehead nestled into the nape of his grandfather's neck. He was not alone.

CHAPTER 10

Russell Copeland

THE EVENING BROUGHT WITH IT the moon, now nearly full. Russell didn't know why he hadn't been tracking the waxing eye above them, given the heartache it had caused. He was too busy, he supposed, freaking the hell out. Not outwardly, not yet. With the internet down on the island, their situation had become one of whispers, about each other, about what the smoke meant on the southwest horizon (could it be Belize City burning?), and what exactly could any of them do given their own waning faculties from lack of sleep.

Russell found himself pacing back and forth, and then treading in ovals, circles, figures of eight. Even when he wasn't in motion, he felt like a top slowly losing its wobble. What did that even mean? Even though he was rattled, he needed to hold it together. That started by trying to make sense out of the fire at the Cava Bar. The charred remains of their island's favorite hangout had forced them all back to their own sections of the island. No one seemed to have been killed in the melee, although one of the groom's cousins had died later— bare-chested, tux pants rolled up to the knees—from alcohol poisoning.

Russell had gathered up the poor guy's three brothers from various

71

stages of coupling with the bridesmaids and led them out to the edge of the jungle path. He provided a shovel, and they took turns digging a grave. They made quick work of it once they sliced through the roots of grass and weeds. All of the brothers had biblical names—he just couldn't remember them. Something like Luke, Paul, Thomas, James. Was it James who had died? So strange how all the males at the resort were related by blood? Or else it felt that way because of the distance he'd always felt from his own father. The universe was trying to tell him something but damned if he knew what it was. His brain was firing—not on all cylinders but ricocheting in a thousand different directions. Madness.

Daniela was so much better at organizing things than he was, but she hadn't made the trek back over to his side of the island. He thought he saw her after Cava went up in flames but couldn't be sure. He wondered how the bar had gotten torched. Once lit, the broken bottles of hard alcohol had made it go up fast. Was it the pot smokers who'd been out on the patio or one of the fishermen who chain smoked hand rolled cigarettes?

The strangest moment came when Rex, the grizzled owner of the bar, led Marley over to him, leading the teen by the hand as though he were a much smaller child. "If something happens to me, I want you to look after him," Rex said.

"Don't be ridiculous," Russell said.

"Promise me," Rex hissed and gripped his wrist so hard the stars danced and swayed from the pain.

"Jesus, OK." Russell stepped back and almost fell into the pool. "Just relax."

"I won't relax. You need to watch out for Jira. He's bad news."

Russell nodded and managed to yank his hand free as Rex coughed and doubled over, holding his side. "That much I know."

"The tide was a sign. Cava is a sign," Rex said. "I should have listened."

"C'mon Grandpapi." Marley led Rex over to one of the few remaining lawn chairs without a drunken reveler or two or three.

Wolf Granger, posse in tow, led the rest of the wedding party over to the swimming pool. What now? The director strutted in slow motion, preening to invisible cameras like on a Hollywood runway. It was ridiculous enough to grab everyone's attention. Wolf finished his circuit of the poolside lounge by striding out onto the diving board like he was going to take an epic dive. He paused near the end and sat. His legs straddled the board and it quivered beneath him like a nervous colt. The diving board was the perfect vantage point for a man addressing an audience, his back to the beach, his eyes roving the entirety of the resort.

"This situation is getting serious, folks. I've been informed we have our first death. We need some rules here. Some structure."

Russell took that as his cue, but he was not from central casting. He strode in sandals and shorts toward the shallow end of the pool opposite Wolf, like a counterbalance to that son-of-a-bitch, who reminded him more and more of his old man by the moment.

"Guests, we have this under control. We still have food and water," Russell said.

"For how long?" Wolf asked.

"There's electricity," Russell continued.

"But for how long?" Jewel Granger mimicked her husband from a covered lounge chair, the cloth roof blocking out the sky as though she were protecting herself from moon burn. Wolf had apparently planted his wife in the crowd to spur unease.

"Mr. Copeland, you've done your best, I don't doubt that. Extraordinary times need extraordinary leadership."

"And I supposed you believe that's you."

"Thanks for nominating me to be in charge. Much appreciated."

"I did no such thing," Russell stammered. "You're a god-damn director. You deal with make believe!" Russell could feel himself getting worked up but couldn't help himself. First, he lost Maxine to that naval asshat and now he was losing the resort. To be fair, though, he was divorced, and the bank technically owned most of his stake in Copeland Caye.

"I didn't want to have to make this personal, Russell, but you leave me no choice. We can't trust a man who is dating one of the natives. It's clear they want what we have."

"Daniela is my employee, and she can be trusted."

"To leave us and join up with the rest of the islanders. Yes, we've heard how their village was wiped out in the storm. They'll be here before long to kick us out into the jungle. We need to be ready. Gather weapons. Post guards."

"We're not the military."

"Good point, we should protect ourselves from the military!"

Russell searched for a snappy comeback, his anger transforming into blind rage. Yes, he understood that expression, finally. White spots from the standing lamps fogged his eyes. The director's tone reminded him of his father's.

"We need to stay civilized," Russell said, the beginning of a rejoinder but nothing else leapt to mind.

"Your head's in the sand, Russell. The scale of this tragedy is large, something I've been training for my whole life."

"That's ridiculous. You make second rate movies for third rate intellects."

Wolf Granger smiled and gestured to the crowd with his arm. "Looks like we have an elitist here, someone who doesn't respect the hundreds of people I've managed on projects with millions of dollars at stake. All of the people on my crews rely on me for their livelihood. And safety. The studio literally puts their lives in my hands."

"You're a god-damn hero," Russell said sarcastically, and he was starting to become annoyed with how bitter and mean-spirited he sounded.

"Damn right. I'm used to shit going sideways because that's every day on a film shoot. I keep everything on track and everyone happy. Sounds like you'd be a fool to not put me in charge."

"Look, folks, I don't think I've done the best job so far letting you know my plan. I promise that I only have your well-being in mind, and that I'll do my best to protect you, to serve you, and to feed you as long as you are here as my guests," Russell said.

"The fucking world is ending," Wolf replied. "You don't need a nice guy. You need an asshole. And I'm the right asshole to run things."

"Here, here!" Jewel called out from the other side of the pool, having slipped around to another group.

It was obvious Russell had lost the debate and was quickly outvoted. It was a landslide. The only person to support him was Rex, and it looked like it was a painful choice. The barkeep could barely keep his hand in the air.

"I'll keep Russell here as my second-in-command. Really, folks, this is the best of both worlds."

Wolf gestured to the other parents in the wedding party to join him and they gathered around the diving board. The director started discussing a strategy with the "adults" for how to keep the sailors and islanders away from their side of the island. Russell was distracted when the groom's cousins came back and handed him the shovel. Rex pulled a bottle of tequila from under his coat and handed it to the kids. They sat around by where the dirty towels had collected and shared it among themselves. Marley joined in and his grandfather didn't seem to mind. Russell didn't recognize the label, only that it was blue and streaked with blood.

He noticed Marley look at him holding the shovel and it made him self-conscious. He was feeling paranoid, like an outsider in his own resort. Finally, he decided to return it to the hut where he'd tried to sleep on the first night. The stars spooled around the moon, and he imagined he saw a Cyclops, single-eyed, universe specter tracking his trek to the shed. He used the keys on his belt but knew that locks were no longer an impediment to anyone who wanted something badly enough.

The wind hadn't changed, still warm and fragrant, and he breathed in the island. His eyes lost its focus. Between two trees he thought he saw the man from the painting in his hotel lobby, the former owner of the resort. He tried to remember his name, but it was lost in the soup of his memory. Teeth flashed like a predator's or was it a smile? Before he could make up his mind, the man was gone.

Ghosts. This was what he was facing? Not exactly a new concept. He'd been haunted by his father for most of his adult life, even after the police found him dead in his basement with a broken back from falling down the stairs several years earlier. Russell was always the disappointment, the failure, the only child who should have been the spare tire for a more dominant older scion. Even into adulthood, he still helped his father manage his properties, and was treated like an errand boy or intern. Worse than an intern. This is what made his death so hard to take.

His father normally couldn't go more than a day or two without shooting him a snarky message or sending him on some mind-numbing errand that he would never get right. When two days went by without hearing from the old man, it was a blessing. Three days was nirvana. Then he began to question his actions—what had he done wrong to get the silent treatment?

The days that followed were ones that haunted him. The hours when the old man had been in pain, unable to make his way to the sink in the basement to get water, his cellphone left upstairs. On day ten, after the accident, his father's business associate Sam Racine from the ice plant decided to take action. Sam had convinced one of the drivers to come over and break in his father's warehouse apartment, looking for clues. They discovered him face down, having dragged himself from the stairs to the bathroom sink, unable to climb up. Dehydration. The old man had seemed indestructible, and it was lack of water that had done him in.

Sam saw how quickly Russell sold his father's assets, and his eyes blamed him. He might as well have asked, *"How could a son living blocks away have let his father die like a dog?"* He must have caused even more tongues to wag by missing the funeral that his aunt Pamela had set up in the Catholic Church he attended, reticently, as a boy. The rumors had quickly spread to the rest of the family—he purposefully allowed his father to die for the money, for the cash to reboot his pathetic life.

Even now, Russell wasn't sure about his intentions. The guilt was real enough, and doubts remained about how his hatred for his father had made him complicit.

"Did you see that man in the brush?" a soft voice asked behind him.

Russell turned to find Marley standing there, a man-sized boy, already his height, a full six feet tall. His eyes were red, and his face was horror stricken.

"You saw him, too?" Russell asked.

"Yes, it was Jira, the priest, the one who wants to kill me. He's stalking us in the brush," Marley said.

"Kid, I think we're just freaking out. It's probably just the wind or howler monkeys drawn to the smoke."

Up the beach, the wisps of the blackened ruins that used to be Cava still spooled upwards and licked the sky. Marley shook his head, and he opened

76

his mouth several times, but no words came out. A small breeze rose up and whisked the ashes out onto the sea, to the receding tide.

"I've always thought of Cava and Rex together. This will kill him," Marley said.

Russell had never before seen the boy's grandfather emerge from his kingdom of libations. The boy may have just been being melodramatic, but Russell also had a hard time imaging the old man surviving without his bar. Bereft of purpose, Rex was at risk of losing himself, of being *moonstruck*. Yes, this term had emerged and seemed apt, a combination of fever and inward force. Russell placed a hand under one of Marley's elbows and steered him back toward the resort. His skin crawled as he imagined unseen eyes tracking him. They were all being watched and judged, by each other, by ghosts, by gods, by the earth with revenge on her mind, by the very act of believing they were capable of controlling anything at all in their lives.

CHAPTER 11

Heidi Radar

HEIDI KEPT SLIPPING IN AND out of time during breakfast on the patio, a once-human gargoyle unable to move and immobile with grief. Her current imaginary form was powerful but sedentary. The main dining room for the sailors, retrofitted from when the house had been a manor, never saw much use. Most all of the trainees and regular crew liked to eat at the tables on the mammoth patio overlooking the ocean. This was the most private section of the base, with a spectacular view and unseen from the coastline. When not used for meals, the instructors used the tables for their strategy sessions, and to talk shit about the trainees. Heidi knew that Rick missed the other SEALS, instructors and students alike, stuck on the mainland.

Waves licked the beach below and tongues probed the breakfast burritos she'd cobbled together. The residents of the base, now a motley crew of seven, had not sat down together at the picnic table in the center of the patio, but in tables scattered around the edges. She almost laughed but stopped herself. Gargoyles do not laugh. She was in shock from having seen the rocket scorch the sky, whipping across the horizon to an unknown destination. Then she realized others had seen the same dragon, their eyes scanning the vapor trail disappearing in the late morning sky, mouths open.

78

"This is not good," Landry said, in a deadpan voice.

"Just like the meal Heidi made. Was that a fucking nuclear warhead?" Trevor Keith asked, his voice jumbled either from the gauze on his face or from a mouthful of food.

"It was a missile. ICBM is my guess," Clint Jenkins said.

"It may not be a worst-case scenario," Rick said.

"Could be just a drill or a warning shot," Owen Frank agreed. "Our enemies are all starting to lose their composure. At least that's some of the chatter.

"I thought the internet and satellite connections were down," Rick said.

"He's talking about the radio," Landry said. "We're being kept in the dark."

"That's by design," Owen said.

"Chain of command," Maxine added, trying to finish her new boyfriend's sentence and infuriating Rick, who stood up and took two steps toward her.

"At ease, Petty Officer Coslow."

"I'm not at ease, Commander Frank. I think you owe all of us an explanation."

Thus, began a heated conversation that threatened to overwhelm her, threatened to set them all at each other's throats. They followed the volley of words between the two ranking sailors from four separate worn teak tables, each of them paired up except for Landry. The base caretaker was already in motion, whisking away plates and filling glasses with water. Unspoken was the fear of an imminent mushroom cloud. Where in the hell had the missile been going?

"We should all have an opportunity to listen to the radio. You hoard it in the office where you and... your guest... can listen to it," Rick said.

"I don't like your tone," Maxine said, her hand resting on Owen's shoulder. "This is not a debate."

"Agreed. Strict protocols are in place for a reason, Coslow. We are still on active duty."

Heidi's mind was racing as a mosquito landed on her arm. Surely, it would not be able to pierce her shell. She was having a helluva time tracking the conversations around her. The mosquito took its time finding her vein.

Her mind raced in and out of moments in time. She found herself in a Brazilian rainforest north of Manaus, a city that hung on the Amazon River like a snakeskin ready to be shorn loose. She was on a college internship her father had set up for her and had driven with her boss out into the jungle, miles from anyone. He did what many men in her life had attempted before and tried to claim her. She'd freed herself momentarily but was scared she could not make the trek back.

She'd been a victim then, but who was she now? The mosquitos on the patio were eating her alive, draining her of blood in a methodical fashion.

"Our mission has changed," Rick said. "Our mission is survival."

Eyes flicked back and forth between Owen and Rick.

"Our mission is whatever the hell I tell you," Owen said.

"We're at war," Maxine said, cutting her burrito into tiny bites to make it last longer, to pretend this was some fine dining establishment.

"The only war will be in my gut after eating all these beans," Clint said, but no one gave any indication of hearing him.

Heidi felt her essence being drained by the opportunistic mosquito. Did insects not need to sleep or dream? They seemed to have been spared from the fate of the howling monkeys and screeching birds falling from trees, crashing into windows, floating face down in the ocean. Even her beloved dolphins had started to jostle with each other. The humans were becoming increasingly crazy-eyed and unpredictable. Cliques were forming. Alliances were being built.

The night before, Heidi and Rick had gone on a mission to scout the makeshift pharmacy. Their patient Trevor Keith had recovered enough that day to get out of bed in bandages like a half-assed mummy. The guy's brain was still mush and it made sense that he was only comfortable in the presence of that douche-nozzle Clint Jenkins. Trevor tagged along after the base's only remaining trainee and spent the night carousing in the barracks, flinging cards and getting hammered with a stash of booze these two bruh-friends scored by breaking open the lockers of missing classmates. This had given Heidi and Rick the opportunity to sneak into the pharmacy. They hunted for antibiotics to help treat a cut Rick had gotten a few days earlier running on the beach. When that proved fruitless, they looked for anything that would help them navigate their current state of unsleep. They'd retrieved two unmarked bottles with one hundred white tablets each. These were meant to be combat enhancers. It was some form of speed, Heidi was sure of it, having had her own addiction back when she danced for men and her own demons.

Speed was a double-edged sword, dangerous enough in the best of times. Heidi'd learned that you needed to listen to your own body, to understand when your heart was racing too much and the signs of exhaustion. Between the stress of survival and the never-ending tiredness, you risked having a heart attack or stroke. Then again, if you weren't alert, you risked losing your edge in an environment where friends and foes were difficult to discern. So, the go pills were a calculated risk. They each downed one.

She and Rick had been wired and chatted away all night on the beach beside the moored boats, discussing what they would do when the catastrophe was over. The dolphins chattered frantically beside them, but the noise was background, like the waves, and the wind whipping along the creaking tin roofs. They had reminisced about family, no one close either in proximity or emotionally, and the terrible decisions they'd made in their lives. Just before dawn, Heidi had led them on another raid. This time in the kitchen to make breakfast for the base: burritos with powdered eggs, stale tortillas, and the remainder of the bacon in the cooler. Most of the perishables were gone, but the meat locker still held enough food for weeks. And there were always the MREs, meals ready to eat, that the trainees used when out all day on the water.

"We can't let something like a lack of sleep turn us against one another. It's us against the world," Rick said, and Heidi snapped out of her reverie, pulling on sunglasses to hide her bloodshot eyes.

"No, it's us against the rest of the islanders. We need to protect what's ours and information is power," Owen said.

Heidi's hand hovered over the mosquito, and she was brought back to Brazil, remembering the ultimatum from Jorge, the leader of their rainforest sanctuary. Their work was paid for by tourists, and she soon put aside any thoughts that she would learn anything substantive toward her Zoology degree. Her summer internship had been to nurse injured animals back to life, but she spent most of it running errands, playing tour guide, cleaning up for the staff. When Jorge had taken her out to return a mustached tamarin they'd nursed to health back to the jungle, she had no idea what she would be asked to do. His choice for her was simple: either he would take her from behind or he would leave her behind with the tamarind. She was scared but had tried not to show it. It was a mosquito that landed on her arm that had made her choose life. Choose the pain. Choose the humiliation of working there another month before heading home while that monster pretended nothing was out of the ordinary.

She was coming down from the speed, that was all. She'd gone deep down into the well of her thoughts. Her hands were sweaty, shaking, as she popped the cap on the plastic bottle in her shorts and slipped two pills in her palm. She dry-swallowed them and slapped the mosquito. There was smoke, not from the kitchen. She stood in alarm.

"There's something wrong here," Heidi said.

"That's an understatement," Trevor Keith mumbled through the bandages.

"We got two bucks locking horns," Clint said. He looked as lost in his own world as she'd been earlier.

While she was daydreaming, Rick had crossed the terrace and was face to face with Owen. The Commander had drawn a pistol and was pointing it at Rick's feet.

"Stand down," Owen said.

"This is about more than following orders," Rick countered.

"This is a warning," a voice boomed from the courtyard.

Heidi was first to race into the kitchen. She ducked out into the hallway and sprinted toward the front door. She shouldered it open and stood at the top of a wide double stairway curving down to the driveway. From this vantage point she could see the base's two Humvees parked on either side of the flagpole. The metal gate, surrounded by stone turrets, featured thick metal bars, but it was still possible to see Jira pressed up against it. The island preacher held what appeared to be a bullhorn fashioned from a coconut to his lips. Behind him, a group of villagers hung back from the gate, and it was difficult to discern faces from this distance.

"If you attack us, you will pay the price. We could not let you keep those war machines in the ocean," Jira said, pulling a pistol from his belt and waving it wildly.

The rest of their ragtag base personnel assembled behind her at the bottom of the front steps, flanked by two sleepy-looking stone lions. Heidi could now see the origin of the smoke. Gray plumes wafted up over the water, from the direction of the docks.

"The boats," Heidi called out to Rick. "We need to get to the boats."

"Get off our property," Owen called out, "or you'll pay the price."

"This island does not belong to you but to God. And to those of us who believe."

"I believe you're going to be needing a doctor to pull lead out of your ass," Owen said.

The Commander fired a bullet that ricocheted off the fence and into one of the Humvee side mirrors. Shattered glass flew in all directions. Landry flung himself to the ground and Maxine crouched behind one of the lion statues. Clint backed away inside and Heidi gripped Rick's elbow to keep him from launching himself into the line of fire. Trevor Keith walked over calmly to pick up a shard of the broken mirror and smiled at his reflection. Jira fired several wild shots from his pistol before disappearing from the gate. Owen looked for him in the throng of villagers scattering back toward the tree line.

"The boats," Heidi repeated. She jabbed at the shoreline, at the billowing smoke, and they raced back inside. The quickest route to the docks was alongside the barracks. They heard the ring of several more shots, then two large explosions shook the building, one after the other. Rick grabbed Heidi to keep her from falling. The ground felt like surf for just a moment, then the moment and Rick were gone. He raced toward the doors, one of which was hanging on a single hinge. She struggled to put one foot in front of the other. When she emerged, it was a scene straight out of hell. The boats were in flames from the gasoline tanks, but the explosion had not managed to set the fort on fire. Several holes from the explosion had punctured the building but there was too much stone for the building to catch.

Rick grabbed an extinguisher and focused his attention on the docks, smothering out the flames and working his way to the boats if you could call them that. They were pieces of boats. *My babies*, Heidi thought, and raced toward the dolphin pens. The gate was open, either from the explosion or from sabotage. She peered out to see if she could see them bobbing in the waves but could only make out a small boat being paddled by two islanders, who looked nearly identical, only in different sizes. The larger one paddled in front and the smaller one spun and waved at her.

"This is only the beginning, isn't it?" Heidi said out loud.

"You bet it is," came the response behind her. She whirled to see Clint sipping a Negro Modelo from some private stash he must have squirreled away. He did not make any movement to help Rick douse the flames. "Maybe we should get some marshmallows?" he suggested.

The pills were starting to kick in again. She leaned down and grabbed the bucket she used to feed the dolphins. She dipped the plastic container into the foamy water. The reflection of the flames looked like blood, a trick of the light. Rick would not stop, and neither would she. She continued flinging water along the dock until the flames disappeared and finally the smoke, until her hands were raw, and they both collapsed next to the supply lockers in each other's arms, not caring what the others thought, or joining in the discussion of revenge. *Kill or be killed*, *armed guards*, *hunting expedition*. The debate would rage for the rest of the day over who their enemies really were while Heidi wondered if they were already inside the base.

Chapter 12

Marley Vega

MARLEY JOINED THE BROTHERS WITH biblical names toasting their dead brother James. Even though he worked at a bar, he was a lightweight. He was careful to only down every other shot of tequila offered to him, and worried about fitting in as the brothers told stories. James was beloved but also the frequent butt of jokes. Sometimes the stories were tender. At other times it was like a roast. Maybe it was in bad taste to be toasting someone who'd died from alcohol poisoning, but Marley felt vulnerable. The incident with Jira had shaken him to the core. Other than Rex, he had no tribe, no group, no shield. There was now strength in numbers. It felt important at this juncture to not rock the boat or seem deviant, so he laughed at what he assumed were the right places in the stories, taking his cues from the brothers.

Rex was grumpier than usual and settled into a lounge chair in the corner of the pool area, beneath an awning depicting Neptune spearing a whale with a giant trident. Marley thought this was an odd decoration for an eco-tourism resort. Many items on the caye appeared to have been abandoned by previous resort owners or guests. Rex had told Marley more than once that he was certain the island had a curse, but that didn't faze him as their family was

85

cursed far worse. His Grandpapi had his share of ticks and superstitions, and believed alternately in God, the devil, and everything in between. Perhaps it was his fear of karmic retribution for their family's connections (his father assured them far in the past) to organized crime.

Marley did not know how to console Rex. This made him hesitant to seek him out in the shadows. Instead, he sought solace in the group of boisterous brothers. Because of the tragedy, they were temporarily being held out of discussions on assignments being cooked up by that creepy-ass director .
The night was unusually warm, with little to no wind, as though the embers from the bar were causing them to sweat. The misshapen moon stared down, blanketed by pinpricks pulsating in the sky. The liquor didn't help matters and Marley tried to remember the last time he'd eaten.

The brothers' parents stopped by only once. Their mother was the sister of the groom's mother, and their father resembled his wife so closely that they looked like siblings, like one of those apps that show what you'd look like if you were the opposite sex. Marley mentioned this after they departed, and the brothers laughed. His filter was gone. His companions had lost their boundaries, too. They told tales of how they'd made their youngest brother the butt of jokes, but there was love there, a calloused kind of love. Marley's temples started to throb, and he wondered if his companions could see that he was gay.

Luke, the oldest and tallest brother with a goatee and black stud earrings, ran his fingers through his wispy blond hair. He began telling them a story about the first time that James had gotten laid. It was in their parents' basement and the neighbor girl Katie had dropped over. She'd had an obvious crush on Luke, and he sometimes snuck her downstairs to have his way with her. This was not going to end well. Marley tried to leave the circle to pee, but this story was too wicked. He supposed that meant something good. Or maybe not.

"I turned out the light in the basement and sent James down. He came back once with disheveled clothes like he didn't want to go through with it, but we made him," Luke said.

"We made him a man," Paul said, toasting with the last of the tequila.

"Where can we get some more of this shit?" Daniel asked, rubbing his goatee, the only of the brothers to have brown hair instead of blond.

Marley had an idea, but first looked to make sure Rex wasn't within earshot. "The basement should have survived the fire. There's a bunch of beer and spirits down there."

"Right on, brother," Luke said, his face beaming but this made Marley only think more about how alone he was in the world with his mother on another continent and father too involved with affairs of government to check in on him. Unlike many of the others, Marley hadn't had any luck contacting his father. The Belize phone grid went down early on, and he had no idea if his father had even tried to reach him. On a lark, he took out his phone the first day and dialed his mother, but there was nothing, not even a ringtone. What was Paris like in the midst of this crisis? Was civilization in flames or were people looking out for one another? He was pretty sure he knew the answer.

The brothers stared at him expectantly and he led the way to the bar along the concrete walkway painted with sea creatures, but sloppily. Had some tourist done this, or had it been a stylistic choice? It pained him to see the place that most felt like home in the world was now a pile of charred wood and ash. The outline was still obvious, and he would know his way there blindfolded. He pointed toward the back entrance, where the hatchway was visible next to the metal trash bin that had mostly survived. "I'll stay here if you don't mind," he muttered. He felt clammy and was sweating profusely.

The brothers didn't bother to respond. They high fived each other and raced toward the hatch like they were children. *Watch out for nails and glass*, Marley found himself thinking. Perhaps lack of sleep made adults act young and kids like their grandparents. His lips were chapped, and he reached for a tube of balm inside his cargo pocket, applying it quickly. He rubbed his lips together and pocketed the tube.

"Wearing lipstick?" a voice behind him asked.

Marley whirled and discovered Wolf Granger sitting cross-legged on a crest with a view of the ocean, the resort, and the incinerated bar.

"Chapped lips," Marley said.

"You're not drinking enough water. None of us are," Wolf said.

"True that."

"I'm trying to figure out how large to make our perimeter, and how to protect ourselves if it comes to it."

"Nothing can protect us from our worst natures," Marley offered.

"Maybe not...but we can try to hang on. Copeland doesn't have any guns on the premises except for an old hunting rifle from the guy who used to own the resort before him."

Wolf reached behind him and held the scratched-up weapon in the air like a talisman with two hands.

"Guns are a nightmare," Marley said. "In the wrong hands. And all of ours are shaking."

"I'm not sure this pop gun works but people are dangerous. I think you know what I'm talking about."

"It's hard to know exactly *who* to trust," Marley said and cocked his head momentarily at the whooping of the brother's underground.

"Glad to hear you say that. I was hoping to use you as a spy. You and your grandfather are some of the only natives here at the resort. We need to know what's going on in D-town."

"Jira is bad news. He wants me dead, I think," Marley said.

Wolf shook his head. "He wants you to believe in him, in God, and him as God. One and the same. We are the devils, you see, of Devil's Caye."

"My father believes the island itself is a devil. People have gotten messed up here years before the moon got slapped out of orbit," Marley said.

"I think you need to ask yourself what you're willing to do to survive. As long as you can. My theory is that our bodies will adjust eventually," Wolf said. "All we have to do is stay alert, stay alive, and stay together. You have a choice to make."

"What is that exactly?" Marley asked.

"Do you commit yourself to the resort?"

Marley opened his mouth, a sarcastic remark ready to launch but thought better of it. He needed to keep his options open. To not make waves. To seem like he was not a problem. So much of his response to this burgeoning Armageddon matched his low-key approach to being gay. Stay under the radar. Pretend to be what people think you should be. So much pain and frustration with projecting a milquetoast image. "You can count on me," he responded.

"Good boy," Wolf said.

"I'm not a boy," Marley snapped, before he came back to his senses. He was pissed off. At everything and everyone. But he needed to control his emotions and think of his acting training. Yes. *Project calm.* "This is a man's job you need doing."

"I may have underestimated you, Marley," Wolf replied, flashing him what appeared to be the peace sign in the moonlight.

Marley nodded and didn't want the conversation to drag on. He wasn't sure how it had gotten so late or when day had transitioned to night. He felt not quite human, wiped from the booze and this bizarre interaction on the heels of hanging out with the brothers. Behind him, he noticed a case of wine and two cases of beer had been stacked in a mini pyramid. The brothers must have emerged with their haul and disappeared back into the bowels of the bar. Marley couldn't take any more chatter or tequila. He nodded at Wolf and lurched into motion, stumbling over a dune crest toward a small outcropping of rocks. This was his grandfather's favorite place to go outside the bar. It was a tricky boulder to climb but Marley knew the best handholds from summers of following Rex to watch the sun rise after nights they let the bar stay open until the wee hours of the morning. Once you reached the top of the outcropping there was a space inset overlooking the water—a mini throne of sorts.

This would be the perfect place for him to meditate and try to regain his composure. He was afraid of so many things. Men with claws and fangs. Birds that had begun to attack inanimate objects. Screaming monkeys promising untold horrors for those stumbling into the forest. His hands were slippery, but he pulled himself up to the top where finally he could rest awhile. But Rex had beaten him to their spot. He was slumped over, his head lolling in the arms of Daniela. She looked up and tried to smile at him, but the result was horrifying, like seeing a skeleton smile. Her shirt was stained with blood.

"What did you do to him?" Marley asked, taking a half-step back and almost losing his footing.

"Jira stabbed him early tonight when he was rushing out of the bar," she said.

"Bullshit, he was fine earlier," Marley said.

"That's what he wanted you to think. He didn't want you to worry about him. To blame yourself for what happened."

"So, he slunk off like some animal to die? Without saying goodbye?" Marley asked.

"Every time you tell someone you love them, you're saying goodbye," Daniela said.

It was true. For all of his faults, Rex always had told him how much he cared about him, unabashedly, every time they saw each other.

"I found him here a couple of hours ago," Daniela said.

"Why didn't you try to save him?"

"He didn't want to be saved," she said. "And he'd already lost so much blood. He wanted to watch the sun come up. And he almost made it."

Marley wanted many things all at once, to slide down and replace Daniela in the spot he would have normally sat with his grandfather, to turn back time and let Jira kill him instead, to find a way to survive this sleepless nightmare long enough to face the man who'd killed Rex. How had he been so oblivious? Grandpapi had been acting strangely after he'd rescued him, hiding his wound. If only Marley had been less concerned about himself.

"He was my grandfather, too, you know," Daniela said.

"Jesus," Marley said.

"Yes. Jesus."

The sun ripped a pink wound in the ocean, a trick of the sun rising behind them. Of course, it made sense. The strange relationship the three of them maintained came with a bond, a closeness, that had gone unspoken. At first, he'd wondered if Rex and Daniela were lovers, but he'd ruled that out the first summer he visited. They'd always felt comfortable in each other's presence. Now it made sense. How had she known, though, to find him here?

"The bar was his life," Daniela explained, as though answering his thoughts. "Where else would he be?"

Marley had assumed he was closer to his grandfather than she was, but he was the interloper here. Daniela had spent the last decade here with Rex and his loss didn't compare to what she must be feeling. Not to mention the complexities of having kept the relationship under wraps. He didn't know what to say.

The tide lapped below the indentation in the rocks and a small fishing boat drifted into view. It was being paddled by the two fisherman brothers John and Juan, both wearing rock T-shirts—one *Pink Floyd* and the other *Led Zeppelin*. They had always been friendly to him and had offered to take him out fishing more than once. They'd even given him a Bob Marley *Legend* T-shirt that he wore out his first summer on the caye.

"What's going on?" Marley asked.

"We're taking him to the cemetery in the jungle. It was his last request."

There was a small plot of headstones overrun with weeds next to a ruined church in the island's interior, a place Rex had taken him a least once every summer. This was the only place he'd seen Rex pray, at least he'd assumed it was prayer when the old man had bent over a pew and whispered into his hands.

"I'll come with you," Marley said.

"You know that's not a good idea. Not with Jira acting like an asshole," said Daniela.

"Fucker's going to get his. His days are numbered."

"All of our days are numbered," she responded with a sad certainty that sent chills down his spine. "Stay with the tourists. I'll keep an eye on you from a distance."

"I don't need..." Marley started, but he couldn't say that he didn't need her. He was alone in the world and starting to lose his grip in a major way.

Daniela nudged Rex's body to the edge of the boulder and helped the fishermen lower him into the well of the boat where their catch would normally be stored. John and Juan nodded at Marley solemnly and pushed off from shore with their oars. Each took a perch in the front and back of the boat, rowing themselves quickly away from the rocks. Perhaps they'd seen Wolf Granger with the rifle. That was the only reason that could explain how frenetically they rowed out to deeper water. What the hell? He saw fins slicing through the choppy water. Not possible. He must be hallucinating. Was it sharks? Something worse?

John, in the stern of the boat, screamed incoherently at one of the creatures. He fought to regain his balance and swung savagely at the water. The boat was rocked from the other side as another creature slammed into it. John fell over the edge and gripped the side of the boat. His weight and momentum overturned the vessel. Juan dived clear before he could be clipped. Marley wanted to jump in and swim out to save his grandfather who floated on his face, but of course he was already gone. John laughed madly at the sky, treading water. Juan bobbed up on the other side of the boat, each brother gripping the hull. They kicked their legs in unison and strained to muscle the boat over again.

"He's swimming with the dolphins, God dammit," Daniela said. She pointed at the horizon with a forefinger, nail chewed to the nub.

Just like that the sharks transformed into two rambunctious dolphins circling around Rex. Was this how you passed from one world to another in this land without sleep, ferried by animals playing with your corpse, the parade of the insane that they would all be joining? Marley found himself sitting next to Daniela without remembering sliding down next to her.

"The boys will get Rex, don't worry."

"I'm not worried. I just wonder how long until we follow," Marley said.

Sobs rose from the depths of him and racked him to the core. Instead of crying he threw up tequila into the water, his body shaking, two men yelling in intermixed Spanish and English, the day lighting up the ocean reef in every shade of red.

CHAPTER 13

Russell Copeland

DAYLIGHT WAS COMPLICATED IN THE way people were complicated. Each spin of the sun swung the severity of their situation into focus: the madness, both collective and individual. The daymare far scarier than any nightmare because of the added sense of not being able to hide. Russell was not so much a pacer at this point, but a prowler. His legs were beyond aching as he walked along a wider perimeter than even Wolf Granger had mapped for their security. The brush tickled him like the hands of his mother, a memory from long in his past. Before she left them behind. Before his father blamed him for ruining his life. He was a danger to everyone he ever loved.

And just like that, Daniela blinked her eyes, perfectly positioned on a log so that her feet pressed flat into the grass. He'd almost missed her in the underbrush, his totemic girlfriend. Tears streaking her face were the only indication that she was alive. Wordlessly, Russell positioned himself next to her on the log and slid his arm around her shoulders.

"Maybe we should get a room," he said. "I've been wanting to use that line since I bought a resort."

"I thought you'd go with something more classic like 'we'll have to stop meeting like this'," she said.

"As long as we keep meeting."

"You're such an idiot," she said.

"Can't argue with that. Why are you out here?"

Her face turned toward him, and he saw bruising on her cheek. What the hell? Was that from Jira?

"Isn't it obvious?" she asked. "We're between worlds. We always have been."

"That never bothered you before."

"The moon has reminded us that we are tribes and that we kill what we fear and fear what we don't kill."

"This has been the best two months of my life, Daniela," he said. "That can't be a coincidence."

"This island has been my life. I'm starting to realize that I've spent my time poorly now that my grandfather is dead."

He looked at her quizzically.

"Rex...is dead, Russell."

The strange bond she'd had with the island's barkeep now made sense.

"Don't blame yourself. You didn't kill him," Russell said, and the words spilled like sand from his mouth, disappearing in the jungle greenery. Four days without sleep and his tongue was numb. Even his words had no form in his tired haze.

"I didn't stop him from being killed either."

"That's just guilt talking. My mother died from depression. My father blamed me. Then my father died because I let him die."

"Are you sure we aren't both killers?" Daniela asked.

"No," Russell admitted.

The temperature cooled momentarily with a breeze pushing through the leaves. Clouds drifted over the slanting sunlight, and the temperature dropped instantly. Daniela must have felt it, too. Or else he was imagining the chill, the cold sweats, day terrors. Everything inside him felt like a form of pudding, muscle, blood, and bone.

"You misunderstand. We are not just being haunted by our ghosts," Daniela. "We are becoming ghosts."

This made as much sense as anything. He leaned over to whisper in her ear. It was time to say the right thing. She pulled away, just as a small missile whizzed past his face. The branch next to him exploded and a hail of splinters embedded in his neck. Daniela jumped to her feet and sprinted headlong into the jungle. A lizard bolted from her path and ran partway up Russell's leg before he, too, got to his feet. Wolf Granger pointed his rifle at him and sneered before shouldering the weapon and shaking his head.

"You could have killed me," Russell said.

"Don't be so dramatic. I was testing out the old girl." He patted the butt of the rifle. "And driving that damned spy back into the forest."

"Don't be an idiot. She's one of our maids. She's my girlfriend."

"She is no such thing. She is spending her nights on the other side of the island and *those* people are forbidden on our side."

"*Those* people? Really? *Those* people are in this with us. They are us. Don't you think there are more important things to worry about than real estate?" Russell asked, striding over to where the director stood, his nose inches away from the director's.

"Jesus, you must have failed history. Everything is always about real estate. They want what we have unless we can prove to them we'll fight back. I'm looking out for all of us."

"You could have fooled me," Russell said.

"Yes, I did fool you. But make no mistake: your girlfriend will let them know we aren't easy marks."

Wolf had the gall to use air quotes around the word "girlfriend" and Russell could barely contain himself when the asshole gestured for him to follow him back to the resort. His body ached from head to toe, and he realized he was desperate for another drink, his old demons back in full force.

From their path descending down this small hilltop he could see four people standing guard, positioned in a rectangle around his property. For a time, it had been the parents of the bride and groom, but they'd now been relieved by the three brothers and Marley, gripping makeshift weapons and nursing hangovers. The brothers all had clubs fashioned from timber from the now derelict Cava, while the bartender's grandson had found the old man's cricket bat for protection.

As Russell reached the line of palm trees bordering the resort he spaced out. The trees reminded him of something, their heads swayed like hipsters in a conga line. He was immediately surrounded by smoke, the cigarettes his mother loved and his own compulsions. That was all he could remember. Not flesh but plumes clouding his childhood. The illusory mother and her voice in every woman he'd ever chased.

Poolside, his former guests stared at them as they approached. He was shocked by how haggard they appeared. Shock. Disillusionment. Fear. Sadness. Their eyes told different stories of pain and suffering. Between fixating on his own problems and turning over control of the resort to Wolf, he'd checked out. Nightmares had sprung to life, and they all were dancing with ghosts like Daniela had suggested.

"Listen up, peeps. Russell is an example of what not to do. I found him congregating with the enemy," Wolf brayed as though in a community center production of Shakespeare. *I come to bury Caesar not to praise him.*

"I was talking to my girlfriend before this idiot shot at us," Russell countered.

"I scared away a spy sent here from the natives on the island."

"Natives? What about Marley?" Russell asked.

"He's from a rich family," Wolf said. "He went to Berkeley for Christ's sake. I'm not a racist."

"Just a classist," Russell said. "We should invite Daniela and the maids back over to our side. To talk. To share resources. We aren't enemies."

"That's not true. We have more food. Better shelter. Also, to them we're outsiders. Invaders."

"This is going to lead to more people dying," Russell argued.

"They believe they have God on their side. They're dangerous. Next time we catch your girlfriend or anyone else from D-Town over here we'll kill them," Wolf said.

The whole concept was ludicrous to Russell, but the crowd seemed to rally behind it. Their ashen faces flashed anger. The light seemed unnatural or else his eyes were sensitive to the sun. Everyone else looked hangover haggard and the black circles in their orbital sockets were like bruises from giant fists, one in each eye. He lost track of why he was there, momentarily.

96

Daniela, yes. He was standing up for her.

"You should all be ashamed of yourselves," he said, striding away from the pool and toward his room, now vacant since his ex-wife had moved in with the SEALs Commander. He could understand the allure of everyone in the resort hanging together. It was the recipe for living through all horror films; surely, this was what their lives had come to at this juncture.

"I'm not ashamed of myself, enough," a voice warbled behind him.

Russell whirled, hand on door. Kara stood behind him, her face a mask of lasciviousness that had been plastered over an expression of agony.

"I'm sorry," Russell said. "I don't understand."

"Maybe we can both get back at my father," she said. "Come on, let's go back to his room." Russell didn't know what happened and in what order. He stepped back and rubbed his eyes, tired and undoubtedly red from so many hours of being open. The hue of his resort buildings had morphed somehow from a jaunty lime to an olive green. It was as though the resort itself had fatigue and wanted to reflect the world in drabness or else someone had repainted the buildings like an Army compound from some old movie. He remembered placing his hand in Kara's. Time fluttered. Maybe he was the ghost? He found himself in her father's cabana with no memory of how he'd gotten there.

He was floating outside of his body inside of his body. Kara was half-naked, but he was not really here. This entire calamity in motion could not be happening. Did not make sense. He remembered his psychiatrist's advice during panic attacks had been to find a focal point in the room to break himself out of his cycling. He looked around. On the useless TV, the satellite phone beckoned.

The requests of the woman on the bed receded into background static. Russell shuffled toward the blank screen and reached above it for the phone. He punched in the only number he knew by heart. The line was dead, and he heard a voice, "Yes, he'll hate it if you make a call with it. He's insane about it."

"Are you Nancy?" Russell asked, thinking he's talking to his daughter and seeing the young woman in a bikini shaking her head.

"Pull it together, dude. You need to make that call out on the beach.

Better reception."

Kara yanked on his hand, and he stumbled to keep up with her. The sand was the color of mud with the overcast sky. There were shenanigans afoot, it seemed, and he kept losing the plot. They came to rest on the dune overlooking the resort's dock and the charred bar. A small pontoon boat sputtered toward them with two men on board, but he didn't trust his own eyes. He dialed the number again and this time the phone rang. And rang. He remembered the sound her mobile made above her crib, the tinkling of beeps that he sometimes confused for their landline.

On the sixth ring, a familiar, faraway voice cut through the static. "Hello. Are you ready to come over?"

"Nan, baby, it's me. Your father."

"You can be my daddy, if you're into that kind of thing. Just don't set me on fire this time."

"NAN, this is DAD. I'm here with your mother in Belize."

"Mom left me. She always loved herself best."

"She loves you, sweetheart. So do I," Russell said.

"I'm so tired, daddy. There are animals in the streets. They have teeth. There are people in the animals in the streets."

"Is there anything I can do?"

"Bring a plumber and a samurai. The bathwater is spilling. I filled it so I don't need to drink the toilet."

A boat engine sputtered to a stop and there was a scraping noise on the dock.

"Nan, are you OK?"

"And the sword will come in handy for the fuckers at the door."

"Nan, I love you. I'm so sorry."

Russell sensed a crowd gathering and wondered if it was Wolf leading a mob up from the resort to tear him limb from limb for wandering off with his satellite phone.

"Daddy, it's OK. See you soon. We'll meet on the moon with the other angels."

"Nan, take care of yourself. Eat. Stay away from people. From drugs."

"Knock three times, then two, then one, and I'll let you in."

With that the phone went dead. He dialed again but no answer, no voicemail. Just endless ringing. There was endless ringing in his ear.

"Who the hell are you?" Kara asked. He'd forgotten that she was still standing next to him.

Good question. "I don't know," Russell said before noticing the approaching figure rising up from the dunes like a wraith.

"I'm in charge," said a tall man with intense dark eyes, chiseled chin, and skin the color of mud in the ragged remains of what looked to be an expensive Italian pin stripe suit. Next to him stood a bearded mountain of a man, with dark brown skin, in a red tracksuit, gripping a handgun and sneering beneath a makeshift patch that covered one eye. Russell blinked in rapid succession, hoping they would disappear. No such luck.

"Are you pirates?" Russell asked.

"Yes," the bearded man snorted, holding out his non-gun hand.

Russell placed the satellite phone into the large palm and the bulky device transformed to normal size in that imposing mitt.

"Don't you fucking do that, Russell," Wolf called out, running along the beach with the rifle above his head like one of the SEAL trainees.

"You're going to want to drop that old-piece-of-shit gun," the businessman stated matter-of-factly. "Unless you want to be spitting blood out of where your mouth used to be."

"I'm Wolf Granger. You know, the famous Hollywood producer-director, so I'm in charge here."

Behind him the whole of the resort had emptied out to take a look.

"I'm Gibraltar Vega and *I'm* in charge. I'm your worst nightmare," the man said, draping his pinstripe jacket over Russell's arm.

This was ridiculous. Everyone was treating him, on his resort, like the butler.

"Fuck you," Wolf said.

Gibraltar nodded and his burly companion pointed and fired a round into the sand right at Wolf's feet. The director yowled like he'd been hit and dropped the rifle, continuing to dance like more bullets were flying at him before collapsing in the sand, hands over his head.

The crowd laughed nervously, all except for Marley who sprinted toward

Gibraltar and hugged his father desperately around the waist.

"It's OK, son," he said. Where's Grandpapi?"

"He's dead. Jira killed him."

Russell's arm felt suddenly leaden, but he wasn't about to move it. He had a job to do. Hold the jacket. Check. Gibraltar ignored him and coldly appraised the tourists. "Which one of you is Jira?"

"Which one of you is dead?" the bearded man added.

"He's on the other side of the island. With the rest of the locals," Russell said, not sure why he so quickly had succumbed to a new leader of his resort.

"There's going to be hell to pay," Gibraltar said.

Of that, Russell had absolutely no doubt.

CHAPTER 14

Heidi Radar

To climb the outcropping of rocks just north of the SEAL compound, first you had to cross into the ocean from the edge of the dolphin pens. The water was chest deep and the footing was treacherous. A series of handholds allowed you to pull yourself up to a shelf. Dripping wet, you then traversed a rock path that led upward. The path widened the further up you went until you could walk side by side with your companion *or lover* to a point where it was possible to see both D-Town and the SEAL compound edging away acutely from one point of the triangular island. The clouds were lower, the sun lower; even the invisible wounded moon was closer to your heart.

Heidi rested at the top of the outcropping on one knee and tried to catch her breath. This was a journey she'd taken once before with Rick when they first dated. It had seemed exhilarating and a bit dangerous, like any new love. Now this climb had become even more treacherous with intermittent cold sweats and spasms, side effects of their tiredness that the go pills only seemed to exacerbate. *Focus. Stay on the task at hand. Don't imagine yourself to be yet another mythic creature, this time a giant frog looking for a prince to give her wings, to escape the boundaries of land and sea.* What the hell was wrong with her self-esteem? Really? A damn frog, that's what she felt like in her worst moments. The men in her life had chewed her up and spit out some sort of amphibian, a transitory creature that was not one thing or another. If it wasn't her boyfriends, it was the men she'd dry-humped for cash during lap dances, the too-many mouths of need-creatures breathing down her neck.

Or was it the wind? The breeze had picked up at this altitude, blowing along the moss that grew on the rocks, the environment too harsh for trees and bushes to find root. The birds had been plentiful on previous visits, but the lack of sleep had driven them crazy, and she had seen fewer and fewer on the island in recent days. She wondered if it was harder for them to catch fish and insects. Just where was the line that separated animals that dreamed from those that didn't? Did giant frogs dream? She stood and waited for her prince to kiss her, but Rick was busy. He had hauled a backpack up here, along with a rifle slung over his shoulder. He slid off both straps once they'd reached the small clearing at the top. This was no picnic. This was recon.

From this vantage they could see the island stretch out from one of the points of the triangle-shaped island. The beaches splayed on either side of her, one running east of the SEAL base to the resort. To the northwest, the ragged coastline that had swallowed D-town in the last storm had receded, leaving wreckage behind. The only buildings visible were the D-stop store and Thunderdome, along with a couple of huts on the outskirts where they kept the chickens. Everywhere else was jungle except for a cliff on the east side of the island. This rock formation contained caves that only the locals knew how to navigate. Rick stared through the sights of his sniper rifle and settled the stock into his shoulder. For a moment, she thought he might pull the trigger, hoping to assassinate the man who'd attacked their compound. Instead, he clicked the safety and passed it over to her.

Heidi squinted and tried to get a sense of the vibe down below. The daily bonfire that was built for communal cooking and congregation was already stoked and pushing smoke into the sky. She did not see Jira but noticed a couple of the fishermen on the periphery as guards gripping pole-spears, oars, cudgels. They were on high alert. Jira was noticeably absent, probably inside the D-stop doling out supplies and advice to those who gave him loyalty and support. There was laughter and raucous conversation audible even from this distance, unlike their own hushed demeanor at the compound after the explosion. One of the women her age, Lilian, appeared with a bushel of vegetables. Probably delivering goods from the small farm she tended. She wearily set down her burden and shuffled away before others could draw her into their circle.

Heidi remembered how one night she'd hung out with Lilian. The strange event had transpired after she'd abandoned the asshole who'd taken her to Belize on vacation but before she started working with the dolphins. She had spent nearly a week running up her tab at Cava and Lilian had uncharacteristically pulled up a chair to join her. Both women found they had a lot in common, even though they were from two different worlds: city vs. island upbringing, single vs. married, world traveler vs. living in isolation. They had many of the same tastes in music and books, odd that both gravitated to funk and dystopian science fiction. They were both scarred by parents who'd either left them or left them to figure things out on their own.

After a few beers, Lilian had confided that she was unhappy in her relationship with her childhood-friend-turned-husband Enrique. Their parents had been maids at the resort, best friends who eventually retired together on the mainland. The young couple had stayed behind on the island, the only life they'd ever known. This was after Quinn, the former resort owner, had disappeared and Russell was offering low group rates to build up his Yelp ratings. Enrique had been mourning the departure of his friend and art subject, and Lilian was pissed off at him. He'd never shown this much emotion about her. Had the two of them been lovers?

The group at Cava that evening belonged to a group of kayakers who took turns taking the resort's last rental boats out to sea. They were all from Long Beach, part of a group that gathered every Saturday to kayak in the channel and traveled together to remote locations. They were predominantly male and nerds. After a few looks in their direction, a pair of self-proclaimed writers Rob and Morrow headed over and introduced themselves. Free drinks followed. This was always the way of it.

The details were hazy. All details now were hazy, barely separable from the dreams she used to have. They were talking and dancing in the moonlight on the outside courtyard that sometimes doubled for a makeshift dance floor.

That same bar was now destroyed, all relationships hanging in the wind, like her mother jealous of her relationship with her father, like the ghosts of men. She'd found herself in one of the cabanas where she and Lilian had sex with those tourists, and then ended up huddled together. They writhed in one bed, and they let the men join them. Lilian whispered something strange at the end before they nodded off. *Jira really fucked up Enrique. He's not right in the head. God is just a cover for the real devil of Devil's Caye.* It had been so intense. And they hadn't spoken more than a half-dozen words since. Connections were so fleeting in this world.

"Stop," Rick said, and she looked down to see that her thumb had flicked off the safety, the cross of the scope squarely on the entrance to the D-stop. She was ready, she supposed, for all hell to break loose. Ready for revenge. Ready for something. He placed a hand on her shoulders and released the rifle from her grip.

"They don't look ready to attack us," he said. "I need to go, baby."

"What do you mean?" she asked, even though she'd seen him pack up at the base and had already removed his wetsuit from his rucksack. Heidi had finally transformed her prince into a frog like herself. He yearned to return to the water, leaving her to flop around on land.

"Don't do this. You are the only thing keeping us from falling apart," she said, but the subtext was clear. He was the only thing keeping her from falling into pieces or floating away into sea mist.

"They're my squad. My responsibility," Rick said. "They always stay at the same hotel on the mainland."

"Everyone who leaves doesn't come back," Heidi said.

"There's a war brewing. We need allies. Things are going to get much, much worse."

"You're in no condition to do this," she said.

"Not true. It's seven miles straight across to Vista Del Mar. I can do this but I'm not sure for how much longer. Also, I need antibiotics. The pharmacy is in town right next to the hotel."

"I'll never see you again."

"I'll be back. I promise," Rick said, and for a moment she believed him. "I can't lose more men. I wouldn't be able to live with myself."

She thought about begging but refused. He could decide what was important for himself. The two giant frogs kissed, and Rick walked to the edge and jumped into the ocean. He hung in the air seemingly for an eternity before slicing into the green water. She saw him bob to the surface and start swimming westward without looking back or waving.

What to do with the rifle? Her hands shook as she slung it over her shoulder. She had a version of the shakes, the DTs. Something she'd learned from her time as a junkie-in-training was that the spasms didn't come when you quit the hard stuff but because you were trying to catch up on REM. You couldn't dream properly as an alcoholic and the dreams forced themselves out of you, leading to quivers and hallucinations. They were all on a massive bad drug trip caused by their own minds and the demons that roosted there.

Heidi could barely keep it together enough to descend the way she came with the rifle slung over her shoulder. What fresh hell would be waiting for her below? She now understood what it was like to sleepwalk with open eyes, able to remember only snatches of her trip back, like hiding the rifle in the dolphin pen, tucked away in the now-empty bait box.

She hopped back inside the compound, a frog returning to her psychotic dysfunctional lily pad. She hurried past the barracks where Clint and Trevor huddled together like siblings hatching some grand conspiracy. They did not yet know that Rick had left them, and she wasn't about to share that tidbit. He was one of the only things that kept this powder keg from blowing sky high.

A couple of other figures huddled together in the living room. This room had always made her feel at home when the trainees gathered over video games, with good-natured ribbing, beers, and shit talking. The light of the TV had warmed her on many nights with men as close as brothers vying to be top dog. There had been no games of any kind in her home, her mother usually too stupefied from smoking dope after her shift as a dental hygienist to pay her any heed. And she did not bring any of her friends into this world. Her earliest memory was always departure, even in her hometown when she struggled to graduate from UCLA while stripping to pay her way.

Owen gripped the controller and was playing some sort of wrestling video game on the TV. Landry cheered him on intermittently, but his eyes were glassy and unfocused. Could he be on drugs or was he just zoned out? Owen's wrestler appeared to be a giant bearded white guy with tribal tattoos, no shirt, and leather pants. This monster was beating on a black wrestler seemingly half his size. Owen kept yelling, "Fuck you, Jira," as he picked up a bat and proceeded to beat his opponent over and over again. This was messed up, even for the creepy Commander.

Heidi was paralyzed with fear and dread. She wanted to scream and destroy the controller but was afraid to wade into the fray. Owen's face had such hatred that she imagined getting beaten to a pulp while Landry watched. She was horrified, on autopilot, when she raced frantically around the room, yanking the portraits of men she didn't know off the walls and destroying the frames by slamming them against the furniture. Glass rained down around her, and Owen didn't even notice, intent as he was on wrecking the black wrestler, now bleeding from his forehead. She collapsed in the corner after checking to see if she was cut. It was a miracle that she hadn't harmed herself. The afternoon was still young, but she was now older than the hills.

She breathed in and out deeply, remembering how she had done something similar when she'd moved out of her mother's house, never to return. Only that time the artwork had been her mother's surreal desert landscapes she'd painted after work before balling up in a stoned stupor.

Heidi had made sure to ravage her mom's favorite pieces when she left home and she realized that it was because she had been torn to pieces by her father, first by his departure, then by her mother's blame and withdrawal. So much was leaking out of her she felt like she could light the room with the sizzling of her soul. The wall quivered behind her, and she realized it was Landry's hand on her back. He'd plopped down on the floor beside her without her noticing. She felt guilty suddenly for not having stopped to check on Trevor's bandages. There was something about Clint, and the two of them together that made her feel uneasy. She smelled ganja, and perhaps it was the ravaged art that brought back memories, the perfume of her childhood drifting toward them from the barracks.

"Are you OK?" Landry asked.

"No. None of us are."

"Die, die, die," Owen growled at the TV.

106

"Where's Rick?" Landry asked.

"Doing his own thing. Slaying dragons. SEAL shit."

"This place was much different before the Navy purchased the property. Did you know I was here before any of the staff and trainees arrived?"

"No," Heidi said, the scent of marijuana becoming, if anything, stronger in the stale air. Why had they shut all of the windows? As if that act was making them any safer.

"The former resort owner Quinn sold it after losing all his money gambling. He would bring big rollers in from the mainland and host the games in this very room."

"Why are you telling me this?" Heidi asked.

"Listen, I was a slave to that son of a bitch. He blackmailed me after I accidentally killed someone here on the caye. It was more than a decade ago. It was an accident, but I feared I would be charged with murder. Quinn made it all go away but kept the proof to hold it over my head. It took me forever, but I ruined him. I made sure he lost big in those games."

"That's all in the past," Heidi said, the intensity of Landry's voice filling her with dread. He wasn't a frog like herself but a spider in a web that had ensnared him.

"The past is the present is the future," Landry mumbled. "Quinn sold this place and then went under with the resort, too. He went native, went crazy, went drifting island to island. After all these years I couldn't move on. I just stayed here and started working for a new piece of shit."

Landry motioned with a gun finger toward Owen Frank and pulled an imaginary trigger. He laughed and it seemed to pull the scent of pot from the air. Even the light dimmed, sucked into his ashen face. The spider was among them and this one was a patient sort, poisonous, but seemingly less dangerous than the other fucked-up men here. What in the hell was she doing? She was caught between worlds, unable to hop to safety. She absently ran her fingers through Landry's hair, and he closed his eyes and smiled. They were all such a fucked-up mess, and it was only going to get worse.

CHAPTER 15

Marley Vega

GIBRALTAR'S APPEARANCE ROCKED MARLEY TO the core. His father quickly took charge. That's what he did. He got the lowdown on the destruction of Cava and his father's death, and the general lay of the land. Revenge against Jira could wait, at least, until Gibraltar consolidated power. He positioned his bodyguard Puma to watch the door at the lobby cabana where he now held court. Marley now noticed the Puma-branded tennis shoes and red tracksuit worn by the bearded bodyguard. He didn't know whether the man donned the apparel because of the nickname or if he got the nickname because he wore the apparel. Regardless, Puma was vaguely familiar among the dozen or so men his father employed for managing his affairs. Even though the family had gone legit, or so he said, they still kept the trappings of their criminal past. This included having really scary dudes on the payroll.

Gibraltar found a small room behind the check-in stand and was surprised to discover monitors hooked to cameras overlooking the perimeter of the facility. Marley hadn't known this room even existed and this was shocking given how well he thought he knew every cranny of the resort. His father assigned Russell to figure out how to get the equipment working again. "I always thought this was a waste of time," Russell explained. "I hooked up the surveillance system when I first took over the place before I realized there was absolutely no reason for it."

"Now there is?" Marley asked.

"Your father thinks so. I already feel better knowing that asshole Wolf isn't in charge."

Marley clutched the satellite phone his father had handed him and almost dialed his mother's number. But he wasn't sure he could handle the rejection if she didn't want to talk to him or was losing her mind. Instead, he focused on the middle-aged resort owner yanking on wires and turning knobs. The guy looked beaten down and, like all of them, sparring with invisible monsters.

"Why did I think this would work?" Russell mumbled. " I fuck up everything I touch. The moon is probably my fault, too."

Still, he seemed decent enough, and quite different from the former owner Quinn, a man Rex hated with a passion. Marley now remembered how Quinn used to lavish attention on him whenever he came to visit his grandfather on the island. Here, at least, Enrique's painting of the naked dude wasn't staring at him. That portrait was a built-in audience, he supposed, for his father now grilling the tourists in the lobby.

Marley opened the door a crack so he could listen in and found Gibraltar making a pitch to Kara, refusing to call her by her preferred pronunciation even though she'd corrected him on the awkward walk back to the resort.

"All I'm suggesting is that you stay here with me while I interview the rest of your wedding party," his father said in a tone that was anything but a suggestion.

Marley and his mother always assumed Gibraltar had dirty business to attend to and probably the less they knew the better. This made them a family unit without cohesion, on multiple continents, with awkward and sporadic communication. They were all together for no more than few days each summer in a bizarre syzygy of elemental grief, three celestial bodies forming a loose line occasionally thanks to a kind of gravitational pull. He and his mother orbited the planet of Gibraltar, and this rock was now careening off its axis, along with the rest of the universe.

"You make a compelling case," Kara said.

"I need to know who to trust and how to deal with the other groups on the island, starting with that SEAL base."

"My fiancé...former fiancé...is still there, recovering from a boating accident. They only have a skeleton crew there."

"I like the way that sounds. *Skeleton*."

The eight monitors buzzed and flickered on, showing the perimeter of the resort. The images were grainy, tinged yellow either from the old equipment or poor color calibration. One camera pointed at the jungle path leading toward D-town and Marley thought he spotted Grandpapi staring back at him with sad eyes. Back from the dead. Or else Rex had never actually departed this island purgatory of sadness and regret. His mouth was moving, and he looked scared, even before a pack of howler monkeys suddenly swarmed him. He fought them off, before slowly being dragged out of sight.

Everything was a Marley-shaped blur after that. He dashed out of the resort lobby, shouldering Puma out of his way. Somehow, Grandpapi's cricket bat made its way into his hands—he couldn't remember picking it up—and he raced past Paul, one of the 3 remaining brothers on guard duty, not stopping to explain himself. He launched himself into the woods where he'd seen Rex disappear. Surely, Paul must have, too. "C'mon," he yelled. The hoots of the monkeys were epic. It didn't take long to find the melee. One creature in the middle fought for his life, and Marley didn't think twice about it. His fear of animals melted away in his desperation and anger.

"Grandpapi!" he howled, and the tiny heads turned, targets for his bat. His father would have been proud. Never known as much of an athlete, Marley waded through the throng and made contact with his first three swings. Blood sprayed into his eyes, on his clothes, coloring the jungle like a bloody Jackson Pollack painting. He was an unstoppable force against flesh and bone and teeth. Those damn teeth.

Finally, the creatures cleared out except for those he'd downed. A mangled body remained behind with broken limbs on the forest floor, but it was not his grandfather. It was a howler monkey. The pack had attacked one of its own. What was wrong with him? What was wrong with the world?

Time jumped again and he found himself sitting on the top step leading to the shallow end of the pool, feet splashing beneath the surface, droplets of blood mixing with the chlorine. This was the kiddie pool, no shark in the waters as the tourists no longer splashed away, choosing instead to suck up the stash of booze saved from the basement of Cava. No one bothered him and that was fine with him.

A procession of guests streamed poolside to and from the small resort lobby, each led by Kara. She, apparently, had joined his father's team. The first interviewee had been Stacy, her diminutive bridesmaid, as close to a human version of Tinkerbell as you would ever find. Marley didn't trust himself to look at her too hard—he half expected her to float above the ground. Meanwhile, Wolf, the Hollywood director, looked like he'd aged ten years in a single day, the light gone from his eyes as he lay on the diving board, soaking in the sun, trying to burn himself to a crisp, perhaps. His daughter had betrayed him, and he was the worse for wear.

Marley squinted and looked out toward the dock, the tide redefining the beach farther out, his memories of this view overtaking reality. For a moment, Cava was back from the ashes, in its heyday, lights streaming from the windows, seemingly always open. He was carried back to his first trip to the island, not long after Rex had retired here, his bandages from the dog attack still fresh.

It was also the last family trip he'd taken with his father and mother. They'd stayed not at the resort but as a guest at the manor, before it had been converted to a SEAL base. His father had been a business associate of the owner Quinn and they'd stayed in one of the upstairs rooms. His mother kept berating his father for his affair with Nanny Frida, recently sent packing. He remembered the anger and verbal sparring more than the words themselves, and occasionally the impact of flesh on flesh, and his mother crying.

On their last day, they'd gone on a boat tour for them to snorkel. His parents didn't accompany Marley when the instructor took him out into the water. They said they were tired, and Marley had felt abandoned. The reef scared him; it still did. Even tiny fish had teeth like razor blades. His armor on dry land was mostly composed of distant expressions to mask rage with no outlet. He freaked out on the instructor and returned to the boat earlier than expected. Dripping wet, he overheard an argument that left a scar as much as the dog bite over his eye.

"You can't just cheat with our nanny and think there won't be repercussions," his mother said.

"There were. I fired her," his father responded.

"Don't think I don't know about your bastards. Including one here."

"A bastard makes bastards. Isn't that how the saying goes?"

"This isn't a joke. It won't be quite so funny when I leave you."

"I'm going to be a politician. I won't allow it," his father said calmly.

"You scare a lot of people. I know that. You don't scare me."

"Makes sense. I would never hurt you. I take my vows seriously."

"Good," his mother said in a relieved tone.

"That doesn't mean I wouldn't kill all your family members one by one if you file for divorce, starting with your mother and ending with Marley."

"Take that back. Now!"

"I could swim out and hold him under water. It would be easy. A son's drowning would gain me a lot of sympathy votes."

"You've made your point. Don't threaten my family again."

"Then don't threaten me."

"Forget I said anything," she said.

"I won't. If you can't stand being around me, you can spend your time anywhere you want. If you stay around me with this attitude, I can't guarantee people won't get hurt."

Marley was surprised that he could recall as much of this conversation as he did. Was he hallucinating this, too? The bar and memories from his childhood disappeared in the late afternoon haze, sky now overcast. This had been the last vacation his family had taken together. Maybe his father really was a man for him to fear as well as respect.

"Hey, pal," his father said. "What's up with the blood all over you? It's a good look."

Marley turned his head to see his father standing over him, biceps bulging in a black T-shirt.

"Trying to look the part, sir."

"Atta boy."

Really? No 'How do you feel, son?' or 'Whose blood is that?' Gibraltar was just concerned with him looking the part of tough son. At least, in this,

112

he had succeeded, perhaps for the first time. Nothing and everything had changed.

"Come on, Marley. We need to get going, before the sun goes down too far."

Or before the son goes down too far. "What are we doing?" Marley asked.

"Looking for allies. Making a show of strength. The usual."

His father had always been an apocalypse away from being a dictator. He realized that clearly now. Gibraltar inspired awe and fear in those around him. Was it only just a matter of confidence? That and the ability and proclivity to cause harm?

Marley looked around. There were approximately fifteen guests from the wedding party milling around the pool, and they quickly snapped to attention once his father clapped his hands together. One forceful thrum of palms together was all that was needed to roust all of them out of the plastic furniture and stream down to the beach. All of them, that is, except for Wolf Granger.

The director rolled over on his side on the diving board and shot them a bored look. Gibraltar breathed deeply, a mini-Darth-Vader rasp, with no change in expression. Wolf didn't know it, couldn't have known it, but he'd just enraged Marley's father and there would eventually be hell to pay.

Marley was sweating profusely, and his calves ached. The days were not getting warmer, but he was feeling the sun more than usual. It took forever for them to cover the mile stretch to their destination. The group clumped together on sandy knolls outside of the retrofitted SEAL base. They were met with weapons pointed from the second-floor windows and Russell was sent to the gates.

A soldier, with red hair, freckles, a scruffy goatee and rifle slung over his shoulder, approached to talk with him. They both looked annoyed with each other. A man stepped out on the balcony, in a military outfit, gray and black hair waving in the breeze. He projected his voice down: "I'm Owen Frank, the Commander here. What the hell do you want?"

"I'm Gibraltar Vega. I represent the Belize government. We lease you this land. We can take it back."

"I'd like to see you try."

His father may have had the numbers but not the tactical advantage. A smile filled his handsome face, white zipper opening. Jesus, it was a sight. Women had always liked his smile. Marley wished he had even a portion of his father's charm.

"We'd like to make a truce. We're not your enemy," his father called out with a gravelly voice that scraped the sky.

Marley saw the subtext clearly, the revolver in the Commander's hand. Puma's hand on the pistol in his holster. They had heard an explosion the day before at the gated compound and smoke pluming. Marley had been one of the ones to go take a look, but it was impossible to see what had happened inside. Insurrection? Accident?

"Everyone's our enemy," the SEAL Commander proclaimed.

"But we have a common enemy in Jira. We need to bring him to justice. He killed my father."

"Good luck with that!" Owen Frank called out. "We don't have a single man to spare."

"Then how about giving ours back?"

"Gladly. Clint, send out the burn victim."

The bedraggled soldier at the gate shot his Commander a dirty look but followed orders. Russell accompanied him inside the manor, and they all stood awkwardly. Everyone except for Puma, who edged toward the gates. Minutes passed. The ocean lapped at the sand. His father and Owen stared at each other in a seeming contest of wills.

The double door to the manor yawned open. Trevor Keith, face and chest still bandaged, trudged toward the gates, leaning on Russell. He moved slowly in shorts and a trench coat but there was no pain in his face, just an ecstatic look. Did he miss his family and unfaithful fiancé that much?

Trevor's father and mother raced over to him and took over from the resort owner. He leaned on them and beamed happily. He called out for Kara to join him. She took several steps toward the reunion then glanced over her shoulder. Gibraltar raised his eyebrows and his head bobbed sideways in an almost imperceptible no.

"I need you, baby," Trevor half-sang.

She stopped her advance, took one step back.

Perhaps the end of the world should be the test before any marriage. Marley wondered if his own parents would have passed.

Trevor splayed open his coat like a flasher and the crowd gasped at what was dangling there. A vest of C4 explosives. "You'll hurt as much as I do, bitch!"

His parents did not seem to understand what was going on. Puma leapt toward Marley and shoved him to the ground. Kara froze in front of her groom-to-never-be and he pushed a button on the vest. The sound was savage and ripped the belly of the sky. Pieces of the Keith family rained down in a shower, a tropical blood storm.

Gibraltar quickly aimed his rifle and a bullet ricocheted, taking two fingers of the Commander with it. The screams. So many screams. From those who were afraid. Sharp cries from the injured, including Kara holding her bloodied cheek. A fierce war cry from Puma on his knees pointing a pistol at a woman who reached out to close the manor doors. Then there was laughter from some unknown location, the mirth of the soldier who'd unleashed this human weapon on them. It echoed around them like from some revenge-minded God. The SEAL gates slammed shut and the tourists sprinted toward the resort. All but his father and Puma, who calmly stood on either side of him and picked him up. Because of the blood on his shirt Marley wasn't sure if he'd been hurt, only that he couldn't let go of the cricket bat and had a vague desire to swing it at anything that moved.

CHAPTER 16

Russell Copeland

RUSSELL KEPT CHURNING THE EVENTS in his mind. After their headlong retreat from the SEAL base, he'd busied himself. It was better not to think about the seagulls swooping down to snatch up fingers and other body parts. No, he emptied out the contents of both first aid kits and began treating the minor shrapnel wounds. He was able to remove a few slivers of metal out of legs and arms with tweezers, and he almost felt useful again. Kara had the worst injury—her right cheekbone was sliced open enough so that he needed to suture her with needle and thread. Even though he used vodka as antiseptic, he worried about infection. The stitch work wasn't bad, an effect of being handy, and mending his own clothes growing up. Yet another reason his father had accused him of being effeminate but a happy coincidence during the no-sleep apocalypse.

He did all this, of course, because he felt culpable for what had transpired. This was the story of his life. That trainee Clint had acted strangely when he led him inside the SEAL base, making him wait outside the barracks door while he chatted with Trevor. There was scrambling on the other side and metal scraping metal. When the door opened, Trevor's trench coat should have been the first clue. It was a Navy-issue coat and there was no reason for him to be wearing one on a muggy day.

The bedraggled groom stood solemnly and finished fastening each button before agreeing to accompany them. He limped through the halls and out into the courtyard. At first, Russell had assumed that Trevor was covering himself up due to embarrassment, the burns and bandages turning him into a walking mummy underneath his clothes. Russell had a few minutes in their passage across the beach to try to figure out what was going on. He assumed the vest under the coat was some kind of back brace. What he couldn't sort out was Trevor whispering to himself: *"I'll show you all a real blow job."*

Why did so many people drop dead around him? Was he cursed for letting his father die or did it start earlier when his mother killed herself? Exhausted, but wired, he slumped beside Kara who'd been examining his handiwork in the reflection in her phone. He wondered if she could hear voices like those from the evil queen's mirror in *Snow White*. His mind was everywhere. He was having a hard time focusing. He wanted a drink. No, he needed one. He got up and excused himself, still clinging to civility even though he was no longer playing host and there were no pending Tripadvisor reviews.

Russell's eyes darted around the former poolside café-turned-bar to make sure no one tracked his movements. He slipped back behind the bar and searched for where he'd hidden the top-shelf liquor for VIP customers. A small stash was still here, behind the wine glasses. He couldn't help but notice how Kara's maid of honor Stacy was massaging Gibraltar's shoulders. Her wispy blonde hair was released from a ponytail, and it flicked across his face. Women knew their own power. He was certain Stacy was flirting with the new head honcho. Gibraltar shot Kara a *what are you going to do about this* look and seemed to be enjoying the attention.

Kara's eyes rolled back into her head momentarily, like a shark about to feed. He knew that look— his own daughter Nancy had a temper. The similarities between the two young women now became clear to him. He should try to keep Kara from doing something that she might regret. Nancy always had a rage inside of her that resulted in injuries to herself later in life and to those in her destructive path when she was a girl. He vividly recalled one incident on her ninth birthday in the backyard of their first house in Pittsburg.

Nancy was holding court in the bouncy house that he had been reticent to rent for the party. His daughter had wanted the whole space to herself to flip and tumble, the star student in her gymnastics class. Nancy ordered him to keep the entrance clear while she had her time alone, but Russell remembered being distracted by Maxine needing him to refresh the snack tray. Multi-tasking had never been his strong suit. Somehow, he lost track of one of the dozen girls milling around the party.

Asia, his daughter's best friend, got tired of waiting and poked her head into the bouncy house. Time slowed and from the doorway to the house he looked into his daughter's eyes that spoke to him, even then, *"It's your fault, Daddy."* Nancy jumped once, then bounced high in the air. She aimed herself toward the door and flipped. Asia smiled in time to have both front teeth knocked out by Nancy right heel. The strike was so hard and so true that it couldn't be real. Not from a little girl. But it was. Nancy's feral grin before the tears, handkerchief staunching blood, and threats of lawsuit told him everything he needed to know about his child.

Not only would he need to protect his daughter against the world but also against herself. Kara reminded him of her so much in this moment. She needed him even if she didn't know it. He uncorked a bottle and his demons—downing three quick shots. His face flushed with something like courage, and he made his way back to the main pool area.

He tried not to look into the tree line, afraid that his father or, even worse, his mother might be watching over him. Ghosts and people were the same. He laughed at this revelation and clamped a hand over his mouth. Time slipped into a different gear. Somehow, Stacy had made her way over to Kara's table and the two were sitting, glancing around, and whispering like thieves. Had he imaged that Kara was shooting her maid of honor eye daggers earlier?

That's the problem with no sleep. You had endless time to fret and plot and worry. The tables close to Kara were filled, except for one where Marley sat, soaked in blood, clutching the cricket bat. He hadn't stopped by to be treated from the bomb but that didn't mean he wasn't wounded in some way.

"How are you doing, kid?" Russell asked, sitting down so that he had a sidelong view of Kara.

"Not sure I'm a kid. Not with what I've done. Not with what I'm capable of doing," Marley said.

The voice made him do a double-take look at Marley. The tone and the sentiment sounded just like his grandfather Rex. This kid needed someone to look after him and his father had fought his way to the caye to return to the picture. Gibraltar was larger than life and plotting to keep them all safe. But was he looking out for the best interest of Marley in the process?

"We're all capable of great things and horrible things. We just need to look out for each other," Russell said.

"I don't think that's the way we're wired," Marley muttered.

Russell put his hand on the boy's arm and tried to comfort him even as he strained to overhear Kara's conversation.

"Remember what we did at the frat house? It belonged to those assholes until we figured out how to take over."

"That was for fun, Kara. This is for keeps," Stacy said.

"Exactly, girl. That SEAL base IS the best house, the best chance either of us have to survive. They have the prime real estate, the weapons," Kara said, like father like daughter.

"I guess you're right."

"You know I am. I plan on living, don't you?"

"What's the plan?

"The boat. It's the easiest way to slip away and it will be night soon."

"You OK?" Marley asked, looking at the hotel owner's hand on his arm.

"Yeah. Sure. It's going to be night soon," Russell repeated absently, removing his hand from the boy's arm and slapping at a mosquito that buzzed by his ear.

"True that. The moon's more powerful then. It's full tonight and we will all feel the pull," Marley said.

Kara and Stacy rose from their seats and disappeared, hand-in-hand, back to the cabanas. It was dinnertime. About half of the guests had already headed off to the small dining area where the wedding reception was supposed to have taken place. Wolf Granger's sister Regan was there and had made it her mission from day one to take over for the hotel staff and run the small kitchen. It was mostly breakfast for all three meals. It was her specialty, apparently. Regan was thin with large hips, and her shoulder-length hair was purple, dye-jobs like this more and more the fashion among those who visited. She stood out in any room but had somehow hidden herself in plain sight. She made sure to seek Russell out and report on the diminishing stores daily. She, at least, had found a way through this crisis by making herself useful.

He was lost in his own thoughts and so was the teenager beside him. Russell and Marley stared at the darkening sky until Gibraltar wandered over, Puma in tow.

"Marley, pal, I want you to go join the others and eat."

"I'm not hungry."

"It's not about hunger. It's about your strength. Go. Now."

Marley sighed but did what he was told. Gibraltar glanced over at Puma, and his bodyguard followed after the kid. What was it like to have someone like that at your beck and call?

"Russell, I need you to have your eyes and ears open," Gibraltar said.

"So, I'm a spy then?" Russell asked.

"People who aren't any good to me aren't worth my time to protect."

"That's harsh."

"LIFE. IS. HARSH. You have been in a caretaker role and it's likely you'll hear things before I do. I'm only worried about our collective survival. Believe me. We need to make sure we have each other's backs."

"I think you may have a problem then. If I were you, I'd worry about your boat."

"No need to stress, Russell. I have the keys right…"

Gibraltar's voice trailed off and his hand dug into his inside jacket pocket. "My keys were here before I had that god-damn massage." The politician's eyes flashed with danger. "What else do you know?"

"Nothing. I swear. I overheard something outside the woman's bathroom, and I wasn't sure who it was."

"You're a pervert then," Gibraltar said. "Follow me."

"It didn't take long for their new leader to round up Puma, halfway through a sandwich. The man mountain reluctantly left his plate behind and followed them outside. They quickly made their way down the walkway to the beach.

It was obvious something was wrong right away. Flames danced in the water long before they raced up to the resort's dock and noticed that the boat was missing. Night had fallen for real, and they couldn't quite see if it was Gibraltar's boat out there on fire. Still, what else could it be?

A woman groaned, holding her bloodied face. She rose to her feet from where she'd been lying next to the dock.

"You've been betrayed, Gibraltar."

Puma shone his smartphone flashlight on the woman's face. It was Kara, her teeth flashing in the rising moonlight.

"What the hell happened?" Gibraltar asked.

"My friend. My best friend, I thought, hit me with a rock and stole the boat. I saw her trying to start the engine and those…fisherman came out of nowhere."

"Jira?" Gibraltar asked.

"Yes, he was with them. He ordered them to set her on fire. I stayed hidden and must have blanked out."

"This is war," Puma said.

"Yes," Gibraltar agreed.

"I know you'll keep us safe. Now that you know who the enemy is," Kara said.

Russell was puzzled, but he held his tongue.

"You poor girl," said Gibraltar, leaning over and giving her a hug. She groaned, half in pain, and half in some other primal emotion."

Puma stared out over the surf, his pistol shaking in his grip. "Time to fight dirty."

Russell tried to figure out what the hell had happened here. He noticed a lighter lying in the sand beside him. Kara saw him look down. She placed a finger to her lips and winked.

Was it possible? Kara had set her friend and the boat on fire? Was she insane? Were they all? "Kara, you need help," Russell whispered.

"Don't worry, Russell, I'm OK." Kara broke free from Gibraltar's embrace and gave Russell a quick peck on the cheek. "My heroes," she said, stepping on the lighter and grounding it into the sand with her foot. The evidence was now out of sight.

Yes, Kara was OK. He couldn't believe how this young woman had turned into a different kind of Bridezilla so quickly. Still, he couldn't bring himself to betray her. The end of civilization made it difficult to keep moral bookkeeping. Each day brought its own set of rules and who was he to rat out a woman who was just fighting for her own pecking order…and survival?

"You're the brave one here, Kara," he said. This was definitely a young woman he wanted to keep in his good graces.

Silhouettes flickered as people gathered on the beach. News had spread somehow. Someone must have seen the flames bobbing in the tide. The smoke was now something he could taste on his lips. Their ragtag congregation huddled together again. Another tragedy. Another life lost. Perhaps, the locals were right. This was Devil's Caye and the visitors to the island were to blame for the world on fire.

CHAPTER 17

Heidi Radar

HOW LONG CAN A HUMAN live without needing sleep? It was the 800-pound gorilla in the room. Except their conversation wasn't in a room. After the explosion on the beach, they found themselves on the roof of the manor. There was a smoking area up here with empty wine bottles and mismatched lounge chairs accessible from Commander Frank's office via a back staircase. They'd made sure to lock all the doors and sought the highest ground possible as the sun bled out over the ocean. Heidi had given each of them one of her go pills after the incident and they huddled together, revved up and fighting cold sweats and the shakes, hallucinations hovering like angels above their heads. She knew that she was being manipulative in getting them high and chatting but wanted some information. To get it, she would need to blend in with the others.

She imagined herself as a chameleon, and not for the first time. She'd tried hard to feel at home growing up in the phalanx of teenage girls in high school, donning school colors and shaking her ass at the games even though she secretly wanted the jocks and their entourage to lose, to feel the same embarrassment she did. She had been the fastest girl on the swim team until her coach made her skin crawl with his eyes and hands. Her mother blamed her for giving up, always giving up. Heidi was inadequate: not smart enough for the nerds, not pretty enough for the beauty queens, not outwardly weird enough for the artsy crowd. She tried blending in with all of them and wore a slightly different face in all crowds. This was the skill she needed tonight. The chameleon isn't the most ferocious creature, but it is a survivor.

They were amped up on speed and the topics flew by at a fast and furious pace. Her target was Owen—she wanted to know what was going on in the rest of the world and if there was hope for a cure. She'd get the intel out of him. Eventually. They'd already discussed theories about how their injured guest had gathered the knowledge to engineer a suicide vest. It was strange for a civilian to have a working knowledge of explosives, but many things were possible in the age of the internet. Heidi couldn't help but think that Clint had helped him with his plot and the trainee could sense her doubts about him. He switched topics and put her on the defensive by bringing up the subject of Rick. Heidi tried to keep her shit together and calmly informed them that he was out on a fact-finding mission. That part was true. She let them fill in the pieces that he must be out on island recon. It made sense with the escalating conflict that he'd want to get a lay of the land. Her comrades bought it. Enough so that she still felt like she had Rick's protection, even in absentia.

No one dared mention that Maxine had disappeared during the boat fires. It made Heidi more self-conscious, being the only woman, but she tried not to show it. She tried to channel an inner soldier when Owen ranted about how the others on the island were jealous of their weapons, their barricaded fort, and their resources. The foursome agreed they needed to take action and Landry hurried downstairs to dig into the Commander's wine stash and armed each with .45s except for Heidi, who was fine with a hunting knife she'd found earlier in Rick's locker. The conflicts with the islanders and tourists had brought their ragtag group momentarily closer together. Still, Heidi couldn't shake her unease about Clint's character, Landry's backbone, and Owen's sanity.

"It's only natural that people are freaking out," Heidi said. "Five days without sleep and people start losing touch with reality."

"We dream while awake. It's trippy. Like acid," Landry said.

124

"Hallucinations are just the start. We are all now getting the shakes and feeling ill as our autoimmune systems rebel," she said. "You'll start feeling chilly, like you have a flu."

"The Pentagon is trying to keep order but it's all uncharted territory. No one on record has gone more than ten days with no sleep," Owen said. "But this is uncharted territory."

"What about military experiments? I can't believe we haven't done this shit to prisoners," Clint mused.

"We all read the same shit on the internet before it went down. Scientists performed experiments on lab rats to keep them awake for weeks and they all ended up dying without a clear reason why," Landry said.

"Organ failure perhaps. The connection between body and mind isn't completely understood," Heidi said.

The manic looks on the men's faces almost made her laugh and she wondered what she herself must look like.

"The sky pulsates like a heart," Owen said, pulling out his gun and aiming at stars.

The others ignored this non sequitur.

"If we're on borrowed time, why don't we take what we want? Do what we want?" Clint asked.

This was the moment Heidi had been waiting for. "I bet you that our Commander has heard some news about this?"

"There's unconfirmed reports of a few people who have slept by getting used to the moon's new rhythm," Owen said, finally giving them insight into some of the conversations he'd been having over the radio at odd hours of the day and night. "We've invaded a few countries to get our hands on those folks and any research. It's chaos out there."

"It's chaos here," Landry muttered. "I keep seeing my grandmother's hands. She was always touching me as a boy. They're everywhere."

"You sure as fuck don't want to know what I see," Clint said.

Owen sighed. "When I close my eyes, everything goes to shit in my head. It's a horror show.

"We need to protect each other's backs. Keep on mission," Heidi spat out a couple of military-like platitudes. She was having a hard time not seeing these men for the monsters they would likely become. They would likely want to humiliate her, possess her, and tear her apart. She was hiding as one of them. She breathed in deeply and looked out over the water, wondering if Flo and Jet had managed to sleep, if they had adjusted to the cycle of the moon. So ridiculous that something so far away had put everything at risk. The writers, for once, had it right—the moon was magical and a harbinger of madness.

The topic veered again to women, and this was as good a time as any for her to make herself scarce. She mumbled *bathroom* and slipped away, hopefully unnoticed. She was drawn to a course of action that was dangerous. Rick surely would have tried to talk her out of it. Even with the go pill still in her system she was having a progressively harder time focusing. Time really seemed like a fourth dimension—lack of sleep made it sweaty, real, visceral. Used to sleepwalking it didn't surprise her to come out of her stupor in her wetsuit and standing on the naval dock charred from the boat fires.

She stepped out into the water and launched herself away from the base, past the pens she kept open for the unlikely return of the dolphins. It was clear where she needed to go—all she could hope was that others felt like building bridges. Out of all of the roles she thought she'd one day play, emergency peacemaker was not one of them. It was the opposite impulse of most of her life, and it made her question herself and the petty grudges she'd harbored over the years.

Throughout her life, if someone betrayed her, she'd banished them by burying them in a place inside her mind. She called it the *human garbage bin*. She'd come up with the concept in childhood and had yet to remove anyone after shoving them in there. Some received this ultimate punishment for only minor offenses. For example, a girl who'd stolen a bracelet from her when she was in first grade had ended up inside the bin. Her name was Yolanda, and she was one of her very best friends. They'd shared lunch every day and swapped snacks. So why had she been so upset by something as inconsequential as a cheap piece of jewelry?

Heidi settled into a breaststroke, her most accomplished swimming stroke. She felt nearly aquatic with the extra buoyancy from the wet suit. She was an ocean chameleon now, a dolphin in spirit. She made a burbling noise in her throat like Flo and Jet used to make. She laughed madly. Completely losing it. The dolphins, at least, would never make their way into her human garbage bin.

Her father had been binned just days ago as she sorted through memories of him molesting her that had risen to the surface. Once someone landed in the bin, they didn't exist. She never thought about them again. At least, that was the intent. Even if they walked the earth, they were ghosts. Insubstantial. Her mother could never understand how she'd gotten relegated to this purgatory. The offense, like the host of others in her bin, was unforgivable. At least to Heidi.

Her mom had been a jazz groupie, spending evenings at a local club in the valley listening to musicians and hanging out with them. She blamed her mother for the affairs that drove her father away, even though he'd probably had them first. And then there were the countless broke musicians who'd hung out in their apartment. She tried locking herself away in her room to shield herself from the cacophony: whining instruments, pot smoke, partying day and night.

She ignored the men, stuffing them each into the human garbage. Finally, in her senior year of high school, she shoved her mom in there as well. It made life easier and assuaged her guilt when she spent as much time away from home as she could. Her first boyfriends she selected as much to have their pads to hang out in as any emotional connection.

This drove her mother insane and to disappear in a cloud of pot smoke. Mom tried to weigh in on her life choices, but Heidi rebuffed her. She leaned on her father for tuition at UCLA and danced for rent money, leaving home the moment she graduated high school. Her mother never gave up, sending her endless emails and voicemails, and tracking her down on campus for one-sided conversations. Heidi was unrelenting in her unforgiveness. No one ever escaped the human garbage bin. The lapping of the tide as she swam was rhythmic, like jazz music through a bedroom door. She hadn't reached out to her mom when she was an addict and not even days ago when it seemed like the world was going to end. Did her mom deserve to be the first to ever escape from the bin?

It was a moot point. Heidi had no way to talk to her and she wasn't even sure what she would say if they spoke. Would she ask about why her mom left her father, if it was because he was molesting her? Would her mother escape her junkyard fate only to be relegated again to the human garbage?

She'd already swum around the rock outcropping where she'd said goodbye to Rick and past the fishermen's boats. She was nearly invisible in the darkness. She remembered that Lilian lived further up the coast and pushed herself now with a sidestroke, facing toward land, to rest her aching muscles. She needed to convince the others, like she had at the base, to join together. They would all die or kill each other one by one unless they decided to band against their real enemy. Death. Yes. Death was real. It was the reason why she kept morphing into imaginary creatures. To fight against the darkness.

Heidi closed her eyes and heard voices, her mother's, her father's, faithless friends, hurtful men, all of the demons she'd bottled up in her bin. Her ghosts whispered in her ears, telling her to stop struggling, to float forever. She found herself on her back in a resting position. She positioned her ears under water but that did not block the gurgle of pleads and threats.

Your body belongs to me. You deserve to be unloved. The moon is your fault because you drive people to hatred instead of love wherever you go.

Heidi looked up at the full moon and the fierce eye trying to hold her with its otherworldly gaze. She would not take this lying down, even if she was lying down in the water. Every time a man or her own destructive nature knocked her down, she picked herself up. The voices told her to end her own life so they could be set free. She gritted her teeth and fought to regain her sanity. She shoved her mother, father, wicked boyfriends, and assholes of all shapes and sizes back into the human garbage bin.

Heidi flipped back onto her stomach, exhausted in every way possible, but firm in her course. She would live and she would do her best to encourage others to travel this path with her. She wondered if her own experiences with sleeplessness from drug addiction made her more resilient than others. Yes, if they were all now damned then it made sense that those previously damned would last the longest.

She swam past the Thunderdome and D-stop, and a bonfire with revelers throwing up shadows in the moonlight. She was part of the ocean. They would not see her out here. Heidi had a particular destination in mind. A single hut remained standing, and light was leaking out of the windows. Her landing spot. She crawled onto the beach and her limbs were leaden. No time to rest, though. She gathered herself and her courage and stripped off her wetsuit. She felt chilled by the night breeze even though only her hair was wet. She crossed the sand, wondering if her body's thermostat was starting to fail her.

Thankfully, the voices of her ghosts had subsided. The lid on her human garbage bin was holding…for now. She stopped on the doorstep. She knocked three times in rapid succession. Lilian opened the door and crushed her in a hug while her cousin Daniela ran past them to see if anyone was watching the reunion. Daniela ushered them inside and closed the door. "You're crazy coming here."

"But we're glad you did," Lilian said, gesturing for Heidi to join her at the kitchen table.

"This is the only hut still standing. We get a lot of visitors. It isn't safe here," Daniela warned.

"Why isn't it safe?" Heidi asked. "Because of what happened at the base?"

"Jesus don't be dense. Jira is convincing everyone that this disaster is God's judgment," Daniela said.

Heidi almost snapped at the insult, but she needed allies. "He always struck me as a creep."

"A creep with a plan. Only a few of us over here are super religious, but he's convincing everyone that this is our caye. *Our land.* Why shouldn't we take back the mansion or take over a resort that pays us a pittance?" Daniela asked.

"We should band together. Rick came over to help try to save your homes from the flooding," Heidi said.

"But no one stopped by afterwards and offered to put a roof over our heads," Lilian said.

"That damned Thunderdome is like a beehive and Jira is convincing everyone to fly out of there, stings outward."

"Lilian, you can convince Jira to stop the bullshit. You have to try," Heidi said.

Both women laughed. "You might as well teach the wind to swim underwater," Lilian said.

"And Daniela, Russell will listen to you," Heidi said.

"It sounded like the resort and sailors went to war yesterday. Why should I do anything to keep them from killing each other?"

"Don't you care who might have gotten hurt yesterday?" Heidi asked.

Daniela bared her teeth, and it was impressively scary beneath her bloodshot eyes. "That's manipulative."

"I'm just doing what I have to in order to survive. I'll do my best to convince Rick and the others to listen to reason," Heidi said.

"It's possible Jira might listen to Enrique. It's worth a try," Lilian said.

There was a brief pause and Heidi used the opportunity to down a glass of water left on the counter without asking permission.

"Dammit, fine. I need to go check on Marley now anyway," Daniela said.

"And Russell?" Lilian asked.

"Yes. We'll see if he's willing to share those cabanas. It would go a long way toward the islanders trusting him."

"Thank you, both. I need to get back. Before my people notice I'm missing."

"*Your* people? Just who are *your* people? Whites? Americans? Women? You better think about that long and hard before we meet again," Daniela suggested.

"Thank you both for listening."

Heidi stood up and blew each woman a kiss before heading out the door. She closed it behind her, deep in thought. She looked around for a while until she found the oblong mound of her wetsuit. Heidi was sore and emotionally drained, but she thought she could make it back to the base before dawn if she hurried.

She placed a leg in the suit and heard the whistling of the oar moments before it reached her head. She tried to duck but it caught her in the temple. There was an explosion in her mind. She dropped face first onto the beach and blinked. Darkness. Everywhere there was darkness.

"*That's my girl,*" her father's voice bled out of her head. She was truly now one of the damned.

CHAPTER 18

Marley Vega

THE DEATHS MUST BE GETTING to him. Or else he was a basket case. Marley began seeing Rex flash into view on the edges of the resort. Grandpapi was spry, leaping off the ground or flinging himself from tree to tree, or was it one of the howler monkeys? His connection with his dead grandfather seemed real, more real than the one with his father. Gibraltar was all business and had huddled up in the resort lobby with his brain trust Kara and Puma. It was nothing new being on the outside looking in. He was left to wander the perimeter of the resort and, when he became too freaked out, to hide out in the lobby's surveillance room.

Even Russell had bugged out on him after the boat fire and the specter of another dead tourist. Marley couldn't blame the resort owner for taking what had happened to heart. The dude was proud of the renovations he'd made on Copeland Caye and had shared with Rex how it was a way for him to get back his family's name. Marley liked the skittish oldster, but he couldn't bring himself to call the island anything but Devil's Caye. This was a name that seemed particularly apt in these endless days of self-reflection and self-harm. Marley was sweating profusely but shivered uncontrollably. He was hot and cold simultaneously. Jesus, he was falling apart.

Time either passed slowly or in leaps. Marley felt a breeze on his neck and noticed the door to the security room was open and everyone had left without him. He leaned back in a rickety office chair and closed the door so that the naked man in the painting would stop breathing on his neck. There were creatures who wished him harm in this world, not just Jira, but that creep certainly qualified. It was just common sense to fear anyone who wielded religion as a shield to mask lust. Marley could sense how that crazy wannabe priest had desired him in the basement of the bar. Jira had burned with a lust and hatred he'd seen before.

At Berkeley, his main exercise had come from fencing, the only sport he'd ever excelled at. Marley had joined an intramural group on campus organized by a graduate student Gary, studying for his doctorate in Religious Comparative Literature. They organized teams, practiced, competed, partied. Marley was in the middle of the pack skill wise but appreciated the camaraderie, gaining a few dozen older brothers and sisters. Gary took a particular interest and sometimes invited him over for dinner or to stream Netflix. Marley didn't think anything about it until one evening when he made the mistake of smoking pot with him.

The memory had hooks and it felt like he was a fly trapped in a moment of stupor and hands fumbling with his clothes. It took him what seemed like an eternity to extricate himself and words sliced through the air. *Let's cross swords, for real.* He blamed himself, of course. He was humiliated and ended up quitting the team, losing confidence in himself, and gaining weight before getting angry enough to demand a duel and draw blood.

His father would blame him for playing the victim. On one of the surveillance screens, he could see Gibraltar and Puma helping a man stagger away from camp. The man in the middle slumped in their grasps—the khakis plus white shirt outfit and bald head belonged to Wolf Granger. Was he drunk? Hurt? Why drag the Hollywood director away from the resort? The men disappeared in the blink of an eye and Marley was left to wonder if he was imagining things. Again.

Panicked, Marley turned off the monitors one by one. He'd been wrong to sequester himself in the security room. He was getting paranoid and couldn't keep his darkest thoughts from swarming him. Yes, there were animals outside who could rend him with teeth or talons. And there were human beasts becoming more dangerous the farther they fell off a cliff with no feather bed of sleep or dreams to stop them from exploding. Like the mother, father and son on the beach that had rained down on them in a flurry of blood, bone, and bile.

The sentries that Wolf had put into place no longer kept watch (perhaps due to the presence of Puma and his gun) and everyone in the resort was congregating at the poolside lounge. The longer they didn't sleep the more their experience mirrored a horror film—hanging out alone was a good way to die, or at least freak out with dire consequences. Hallucinations were shared now like he'd seen classmates at Berkeley do with mushroom trips.

The brothers with biblical names were still sullen from the death of James and playing cards like it was a chore. He thought about hanging out with them at their table but was drawn, instead, to join Russell behind the bar. The resort owner was serving a steady stream of customers from his own poolside stash. Given the rate of consumption it would likely not last long. They were all aware of the dangers of alcohol poisoning at this point. Wordlessly, Marley served waters to the guests to make sure there was some buffer without the threat of last call. It made him feel more at home to serve drinks, in a rhythm like he used to have with Rex.

Russell was less talkative than usual, lost in his own world. Marley had never seen him drink until the moon shot. Whatever inhibitions he'd had before were gone. He was becoming inebriated along with his patrons, and Marley's warning to the customers about alternating with water were directed to the resort owner as much as anyone. Marley observed his father from a distance. He always had an inner circle. Even here, at world's end, Marley didn't rate a seat at the table. Perhaps he was to blame for being standoffish and for thumbing his nose at the old man's gang mentality and bullying ways. His father believed that he was doing right by his son to toughen him up and make him more of a man. The years spent away from home had imbued Marley with a reservoir of strength, he supposed, to combat the collapse of all reason and decorum. He'd learned to rely on himself when the chips were down in far-flung cities, but this pride felt like a hollow victory. They were now all tap dancing on coals and the layers burned and the feet churned, and everyone was floundering with him, and some fell and many more would follow.

An order of whiskey shots from the two remaining bridesmaids brought him out of his reverie. Their names were Tina and Leslie, one pale white, one light brown, both tall and impossibly beautiful with similarly dyed pink hair and dark eye rings popping through hastily applied makeup. These two were college friends of Kara, along with Stacy, and were rattled by their friend's death. Rattled and shit faced.

"Those fucking villagers are animals," Tina said, tossing her hair over her shoulders and picking at freckles on her arm as though they might be removed by expert swipes of her fingernails. "They want to take over the resort."

"Our resort. That we paid to stay at," Leslie said.

"Technically, Wolf Granger paid for it," Marley added, but was ignored.

"The hired help thinks this is a revolution," Tina said.

Leslie smiled at Marley. Her features were Southeast Asian perhaps, or some other hybrid American mix. "Present company excluded."

Why was he excluded? Had they really separated themselves into tribes based on means: the rich, the poor, and those who trained for war?

"There's no they. Only us," Marley said. "We're all animals. We are all hungry. Scared. Lashing out. In pain."

The young women looked at him as though he'd lost his mind, and maybe he had.

"Stacy was a bitch. I hated her," Tina said. "And I hate myself for saying that."

"You're so brave to be honest like that. I wish I could have been the first to say how much I hated her."

Leslie threw her arms around her friend, and they clumsily bumped heads. They laughed and smiled, but it was Marley who felt like he'd gotten a concussion. A dark pit from some dead tree was sprouting in his mind, through his body, and tore open the sky. Daniela stepped out of the fissure, her skin nearly the color of the charred bar behind her. The crowd hushed immediately and several of the tourists parted for her. She saw Marley behind the bar and looked relieved. Someone, it seemed, cared that he was alive.

"What are you doing here?" Kara asked.

The light from behind the bar was weird. She looked like a character from some epic fantasy series striding into an enemy camp and holding a ring aloft. Yes, she was a ring bearer with some ungodly burden. Daniela flashed Marley a smile and he felt momentarily unafraid. He was not alone in the universe. He had a sister, of sorts.

"Guess whose ring this is?" Daniela asked

"I don't think we invited you here," Gibraltar said.

"I found it on the body of a dead man," Daniela said.

Her proclamation had the intended effect. All eyes turned toward her, the crowd hushed, all except Gibraltar who whispered something in Puma's ear before standing up and striding over to face his unrecognized daughter on the other side of the pool. To Marley's knowledge, the two had never met. She was a product from a fling he had visiting Rex one summer and the stipend that had gone to Daniela's mother before she retired had never been discussed. It was a family secret, now out in the open, and there was a lot of frustration in the eyes of daughter and father meeting for the first time.

"No one asked you to invade our turf," Gibraltar said.

"Your turf? This belongs to Russell, my boyfriend," Daniela said.

"Not anymore," Gibraltar said.

"Boyfriend," Russell said in a relieved tone. He and Marley both scrambled sideways toward the narrow entrance to the outside lounge only to have their path blocked by Puma, facing them, arms folded.

"I found this ring on the hand of a dead man in the jungle. Sure no one is missing a husband?" Daniela asked

"That's Wolf's," Jewel Granger said in shock, her hand tugging at her name on a blouse from her "Jewel" line of clothing.

"And you villagers killed him just like you killed that poor bridesmaid," Gibraltar said.

The accusation hung in the air. Daniela looked around, her face registering a combination of fear and shock. "I don't know what you're talking about."

"Girls," Kara said, and Tina and Leslie downed their whiskeys, clanked their shot glasses upside down on the bar, and circled around behind Daniela.

"Move out of our way," Marley said to Puma who stared straight ahead as though he hadn't heard him.

Kara walked in a serpentine motion through the tables toward Daniela. "You killed my father. Do you think you're just going to walk in and out of here?"

"Bitch," Jewel said in agreement, standing up. Wolf's sister Regan sidled up next to her, purple hair flicking the sky, the moon behind it bruised in the same hue.

Russell tried to shove past Puma and Marley joined him. Their combined efforts pushed their guardian back a couple of inches and then the burly man bent his knees and refused to budge.

"Are you really going to let them hurt me, Dad?" Daniela asked, her tone sarcastic.

"I don't know who you are," Gibraltar said.

"Figures. I'm Daniela. Your daughter."

"You walk in here with a dead man's wedding ring and an attitude? I don't think the other women are going to let you get away with it."

Daniela now looked scared. She'd become surrounded on all sides: bridesmaids behind her, Jewel and Regan on either side, and Kara circling around to the front.

It was the monkeys all over again. "No," Marley screamed, reaching across the bar to grab the cricket bat. Russell rammed his fist into Puma's midsection. Before Marley could swing, the bodyguard lowered his shoulder and barreled into both of them.

Marley caught a glimpse of Daniela cursing and clawing at the women gripping her arms before the air was knocked out of him. He heard the sounds of breaking glass and wondered if it was his bones. That didn't make sense, though. On the floor of the bar, he couldn't tell where his limbs began, and Russell's stopped. Blood trickled out of the resort owner's nose, and he felt a knot on the back of his head. An octopus of limbs, he and Russell scrambled to their feet.

"Women aren't helpless," Kara said. "We give life, and we can take it away."

Daniela screamed and Marley stumbled away from where Russell and Puma grappled. He could see Daniela being held upside down and dunked by Wolf's female kin in the shallow end of the pool. Marley climbed onto the bar, bat in hand, ready to leap down. An explosion shook the ground. The lights flickered for a moment and went out. No longer able to see a thing in the dark, the sound of splashing told him the Granger women were undeterred and still intent on killing his sister. He had to do something, anything, to save her.

He tumbled off the bar and stumbled in the blackness, swinging wildly with the bat. He fell over one table, then another. "Daniela," he heard Russell yell somewhere behind him. Marley scrambled in the moonlight, his eyes slowly adjusting. He slipped on wet tile and padded on hands and knees to the edge of the pool. He was helped by one electronic eye shining down on him, then another. The tourists' phones all went to light mode and lit up the pool. There, a woman lay face down in the water. He scrambled to his feet to get to her, to pull Daniela from the pool, but he was caught in his father's embrace. It was a hug like none he'd experienced before.

"Let me go. I know you killed Wolf," Marley said. "I saw you in the monitors."

"I needed to drive a wedge between us and the islanders," his father whispered in his ear. "You'll see. It will give us an excuse to take care of the competition."

"Was my sister the competition?" Marley asked.

"Exactly. You're getting it. I'll make a man out of you."

Russell finally extricated himself from Puma's grip and launched himself into the pool. He dragged Daniela up onto the wet tiles and began administering CPR. Marley knew it was too late. For all of them, it seemed. The electricity, too, had failed. The lights had gone out and he was left with nothing to do other than to hug his father back fiercely and wait until sunrise.

CHAPTER 19

Marley Vega

THE LEGS. THAT WAS HIS only choice in the world at this point. Russell was left with the arms and volunteered to walk backwards through the jungle. Marley, at first, thought Russell was being polite but soon realized that the resort owner didn't need to look at Daniela while they carried her body. Russell had turned his head to keep them on the narrow side path in the early morning light and to hide his tears. The animals were silent, and the only other sound was the creaking of wind whispering secrets through the boughs. Daniela's feet were cold and damp. Marley couldn't help but worry that he was hurting her with his grip to keep her from falling, as if a dead body could feel pain. As if she was capable of feeling anything at all.

"She's better off than we are," Puma had told them, keeping the crowd back after Russell fished Daniela's body from the water. Russell had made way for Marley to take a turn at CPR after collapsing from exhaustion. The lights of the tourists' phones cast the scene in an eerie glow until someone managed to light the torches ringing the pool, a prop forced into service with the grid down. Marley pumped Daniela's chest and breathed into her until the morning sun torched the treetops, until his collapse was not unlike the collapse of civilization around them.

Marley kept his eyes on the path so that he wouldn't go insane: with grief, with madness, with despair. He looked at his feet, hoping that the narrow line of sight would keep him from flipping out. A familiar voice in his head ordered him to *square his shoulders* and *march like a man*. This was his father, of course, scaring him straight even when he wasn't physically there. Gibraltar had a habit of pinching the skin under Marley's elbow to correct him whenever he was out of line: walking, whistling, whining. The pain was enough to make him tear up and the punishment was hidden from view. It was effective, though, and he could almost feel his father's ghost hand on his arm. Even now.

Russell led him to the overgrown graveyard next to the abandoned church in the middle of the island. There were several dozen graves with headstones that were weather worn with crumbling corners and vines threatening to pull them back into the jungle. The dates on the tombstones went back hundreds of years, and most of the names had been rubbed away by the elements over time. Daniela had led him out here once or twice that summer to grab breakfast among the dilapidated headstones. There was a freshly dug grave not far from the church's front door and Russell muttered, "This one was supposed to be for me."

Marley had no energy to ask what that meant. He focused on the task at hand, helping Russell to lower Daniela into the ground. He found a rusted shovel nearby and began blanketing his sister with dirt. The church quivered on the periphery. It was a stone structure with green tendrils covering the walls like a second layer of skin and a canopy of trees draping the building in flowing green robes. Behind this camouflage was a rotten wooden door, broken windows, chipped facade, and a gargoyle on the roof holding onto a bent cross. Marley looked down and lost himself in the repetitive motion of moving dirt. He refused to succumb to another false vision. Time leapt ahead and he stopped shoveling with just her face uncovered. It was impossible to know what to do or to say.

"Daniela, you always loved this place," Russell said. "It was the first place we made love."

"I'm sorry I didn't get to know you better, sis," Marley said.

He couldn't stand seeing her face, peaceful in death, yes, finally released to sleep, albeit an eternal one. He looked around but saw no other signs that anyone else had been here recently. What had happened to Rex's body? Had he floated away with the dolphins?

Russell took the shovel from him and finished the job, smoothing the dirt flat and leaning on one knee. "This is my fault for giving up control of the resort. I should have been stronger."

"Yes, you should have," a voice admonished, and Marley wondered if it emanated from Daniela's ghost. Only the voice was dripping with sarcasm, a man's gravely baritone. "I told you that you'd regret taking over my island."

Marley and Russell spun to see the gargoyle, in a tattered brown robe, jump from the roof and slide down a sapling to the ground. At first, he thought perhaps it was a Jedi master or Sith Lord breaking through the chasm of sleeplessness into their world but then Marley recognized the overweight man with gray hair and a cherub's face.

"I've seen you naked," Marley said.

"Quinn, what the devil are you doing here?" Russell asked, hands gripping the shovel, muscles bunched to swing.

"Devil? That's funny. You get it now, right? This is Devil's Caye and only devils can live here."

Marley had heard the rumors about how the former resort and mansion owner had gone native after losing his fortune...and his mind. The fishermen had reported seeing him out on the open waters, living on some nearby island fueled by fresh fish, fruit, and a desire for revenge.

"You're welcome to this island," Russell said. "It's a place of heartache and ghosts springing to life. All I care about are the people."

"They don't care about you," Quinn said, reaching into his pocket.

Marley almost screamed *knife* before noticing the object emerging from the burlap pocket was a pipe. The robed man cackled, plucked a hair from his scraggly beard, and then yanked several leaves off the sapling beside him. He lit the pipe and inhaled deeply.

"I'm smoking everything on this island. It makes it mine. Everything and everyone. This tree is rooted in death: people, animals, plants. And I'm the master of death."

Marley fought an urge to throw up, hands shaking. His knees were gelatinous, and he wondered if this was how dolls felt.

"That's the fucking weirdest thing I've heard since the moon shot and that's saying something," Russell said.

"Yeah, that's pretty messed up, dude," Marley added, feigning bravado and hoping courage would follow.

"I like you kid. I'll smoke you last," Quinn said.

"Umm, thanks, I guess."

"Great catching up. We have things to do," Russell said, gripping Marley under the arm like his father might have when he was younger. Instead of pinching him, though, Russell led him gently back down the path they'd taken, back toward the resort.

"Quinn, where are you headed?" Marley asked, calling over his shoulder, driven by a compulsion he didn't understand.

"I'm getting my mansion back. You can have the resort," Quinn said. "That shithole is as much a graveyard as this place."

"C'mon let's move," Russell hissed and yanked Marley down the path.

I'm not a child. This is what he wanted to say but no words came out just like no vomit had come out earlier. He was shaking, weak in the knees but they pressed forward. Dizziness didn't even begin to cover it. Morning light streamed through the leaves and the designs were like wallpaper. The island was a place they were all trying to domesticate, to own. The planets had other ideas. The earth, moon, and sun had shown them the stupidity of their ways.

Poetry sprang inside of him now as though from a lucid dream but there was no paper to capture it, no words to hold the power, no readers of verse who would likely survive. Everything he'd ever cared about seemed impossible to place into words and the words he'd always cherished were impossible to now understand as anything more than a diversion. Literature or life? Implosion. Was this a thing? Marley felt ill, filled with the realization that parables were no longer imprisoned by art and that villains could spring out of portraits. His hands shook with no cricket bat or shovel to hold, and he felt exposed by the demons hunching in the shadows.

Russell did him one better. The dude let go of his arm and hurled the booze from the night before into the bushes. Both of them had skipped dinner and had intermittently gorged on chips behind the bar. His vomit was the color of sunrise and bloodshed, the preservatives and dyed seasoning now softened and returning to plants that had no need to sleep. They, at least, would thrive as would insects. The world would be reshaped by those who did not need to dream.

Marley felt a passageway open in the jungle, in his mind. He came out of his stupor outside of the resort lobby. Russell paused with his fist outstretched at the door, unsure whether to knock. The building throbbed and the walls dripped a urine color into the air. Marley blinked and slid a cheap pair of sunglasses from his cargo shorts onto his face. *Yes, this was all perfectly normal. Don't let anyone know you're tripping your balls off.*

Puma's voice leaked through the closed door: "I could take out their leader and it would be the same."

"But that's not what I asked you to do," Marley's father replied in a calm tone, barely audible.

"They are our people, G," Puma said.

Marley held his breath and listened. G was a nickname that his father only allowed with his "business" associates. Marley had once used it jokingly and was told that he would need to earn the right by running laps in their driveway with his father driving his Jaguar behind him. Marley had thrown up his arms in defeat before they even began. He'd failed that test of mettle and would forever be on the outside looking in.

"You are my people," Gibraltar said. "So is my son."

"It's going to take everything I have left."

"Save bullets when you can and take those dumbass brothers with you. I want you to send a message of biblical proportions: scorched earth, etc.

"It was wrong what happened at the pool." Puma said. "Even I'm not that cold."

"She was a means to an end. Besides, Kara did the heavy lifting and she's not acting like a lil' bitch," his father said.

Marley and Russell put their ears closer to the door, waiting for an answer, and they got it in the form of Puma bursting out of the lobby. They jumped back to barely miss the careening door and Puma's massive shoulders as he marched outside, swearing at the sun in some unknown guttural language, stomping the paving bricks into submission.

Marley turned his head and his father stared at him expectantly. Kara's face was a mask of indifference.

"It's the rest of our leadership team," Gibraltar said. "Thank you both for taking care of the body. It was a tough, but necessary sacrifice. We needed something to fight against."

"She was your daughter," Marley said.

"She was a mistake. She was a symbol of my weakness as a man. She is now a symbol for us to rally around."

"What are you talking about?" Russell asked. "What possible need did it serve to kill a woman who was too good for the both of us?"

"The fate of women everywhere," Gibraltar said.

"The fate of all of us," Marley said.

"Now that the electricity is down, we need to consolidate power," his father said, shaking his head. "Without mercy. And to do that we need enemies. If we're going to survive, we need to make hard choices."

"Did you kill Wolf, too? Marley asked. On the floor, by the check-in desk, he noticed the director's discarded rose-colored sunglasses on the floor, one lens crushed, the frames blood-stained.

"My hands are clean, son," Gibraltar said.

Marley couldn't help but see the logic in his father's explanation. Others did his bidding. Puma, Kara, and a host of others throughout his life. He was above it all, as usual. Beyond the pain. The consequences. *Would he sacrifice me to save himself?* Marley was not sure he wanted to know the answer.

"You're going to pay for this," Russell said. "That isn't a threat. Just a fact. Someone will betray you when you least expect it. It won't be me, but it is a certainty."

"Now that's the funniest thing I've heard all day. Why don't you two make yourselves useful and help Regan save what she can in the kitchen. We need to prioritize what we eat now and what we ration.

When neither of them moved, Gibraltar snapped his fingers and they hurried out the door like it was a gunshot. Marley made the mistake of looking over his shoulder. Kara laughed and lowered herself to her hands and knees, crawling on all fours toward his father and purring like a cat. They were all now animals. Or something worse. He followed the resort owner in a zigzag pattern through the complex.

Marley heard rustling in the trees and tried to dampen the whispers in his head. *He wasn't losing his mind.* One step in front of the other, he followed Russell and the silence struck him. It was very much unlike even a few days ago. How many people had they already lost? One of the cabanas had an open door and Russell closed it, still a caretaker, old habits hard to change even when everything was falling apart.

They slipped in the back of the kitchen and found the normally organized area in complete disarray. The walk-in freezer and cabinet doors were splayed open, packets of meat exposed on cutting boards, dry and canned goods scattered. The door to the dining room was closed and Marley was startled when he heard a woman's laughter emanating seemingly from thin air.

Beneath the sink, they found Regan crammed into a tiny space, cross-legged, tears streaming down her face.

"I did it," she explained, between spasms of laughter. "I poisoned myself."

"What are you talking about?" Marley asked.

"You boys don't want to be eating here. Sickness. It's a sickness. All those girls who killed Daniela, they're poisoned, too."

Russell nudged open the door to the dining room and saw the other women who'd drowned Daniela eating plates of what appeared to be pot roast, or something similar.

"I forgive you," Marley said. "Climb out of there. This isn't a time for dying."

"Yes, it is," Regan said. "Honey, I don't forgive myself. We're all dying."

Regan's eyes rolled back, and she crawled out onto the floor. She lifted herself up to the level of the trashcan and started throwing up.

"I don't forgive you," Russell said. "Then again, I don't forgive myself. I hope it hurts."

Regan couldn't answer as she heaved into the aluminum container over and over again. Marley supposed he should go out into the dining area to warn the bridesmaids and Kara's mother, but something told him that it would already be too late, if not to save their bodies, then their souls.

144

Instead, he pulled back Regan's purple hair so that it wouldn't get splattered with throw-up and she continued emptying herself out into the trash. This was something he could control. It was a start.

CHAPTER 20

Heidi Radar

ONE EYE WAS SWOLLEN SHUT and the other fluttered open. Heidi Radar recognized the D-Stop immediately, even from her vantage point lying atop the counter next to the cash register in the back of the store. The shelves were filled with your standard convenience store staples but with island flair: packaged goods with the shelves half-empty, a hardware section, electronics supplies, and tourist knickknacks, empty bins for overpriced fruit and vegetables from the missing ferry, and a mishmash of clothing options, from flowered shirts, off-brand swimwear, and even an umbrella and poncho display near the closed front door for rainy season. Morning sunlight streamed through the windows through half-drawn shades like light razorblades and pockets of shadows surrounded her.

I always wanted to tie you up like this, a sultry voice whispered, and Heidi thought she recognized one of her creepier mother's boyfriends who went by Stan but who she'd called *Stank*. The dude had warned her that she would get hers one day and she did get punished, but not by him. She remembered how she'd once allowed herself to get tied up by a one-night stand and her roommate's boyfriend came into her bedroom when she called for help the next morning after her date had taken off, seeing her writhing

146

there, and telling her how she was always flaunting her body for him to see. Heidi hadn't really blamed him at the time for what happened, and her roommate had called her a slut and kicked her out to find a place with one of the other dancers at Club Paradise. She didn't remember the asshole's name anymore only that his dick was soft, and she'd laughed until he bruised her face with his fist and complained how she'd hurt both his hand and his feelings. Yes, this pain was familiar.

She sat up in order to shake her collection of human trash deeper into the bin and discovered that her arms and legs were trussed with rope. Her right cheekbone felt like it was on fire, and she ran her fingers along it, cords cutting into her wrists. Someone had clocked her good and she'd been blinking in and out of consciousness. The pain helped her focus, though. Someone was holding her prisoner and had been stupid enough to leave the knots so that she could untie them with her teeth. She studied the intricate loops and it seemed hopeless—some devilish sailor's knot bound her wrists up to her mid-forearm. Her front teeth already hurt, perhaps rattled by the knockout blow, and she sank them into the most likely spot.

"Wait a minute, Heidi. You and I have some catching up to do," Maxine said.

Heidi spat the rope out of her mouth and looked down behind the counter. Somehow, she'd missed the redhead sitting on a stool by the cash register watching over her. Of course. The bitch must have been the one who blindsided her.

"You're a real piece of work," Heidi said. "I assume I have you to thank for my black eye."

"Saves you from worrying about mascara."

"Cute. I'm not the one that spends hours in the mirror trying to dab away my wrinkles."

"Don't think flattery is going to help you, Heidi."

"Fine. I'll be direct. What's your motive here for tying me up?"

Maxine sighed and stood up; the redhead's face was visibly scratched and bruised now that she stepped into the strips of light. She appeared to have aged years in the days since Heidi had last seen her. Everyone was beginning to look like drug addicts, red eyes, puffy cheeks, dark rings. This is why Heidi refused to look in a mirror. Her deterioration would remind her too much of the drug-addled existence that had at one time morphed her into a ghoul. She'd always thought zombie shows and movies were stupid, but it was just society's way of preparing for the eventual sleepwalking through life. She hadn't needed to watch that crap because she'd already been preparing for years. Perhaps this, and the go pills, explained why she seemed to be keeping her faculties longer than others around her.

"I'm not doing well here. Jira appears to not like women as much as I thought," Maxine said.

Heidi laughed at the honesty and felt not quite sorry for her, but at least a grudging respect. Maxine had seized the moment after seeing how Owen's weakness would not keep her safe. She'd been right about that but had not managed to wrap the local storeowner and preacher around her little finger. The dude was a zealot. That explained a lot of the weird things she'd heard him spout in her few interactions in Cava over the past few months.

"Let me go and I'll help you. We'll make our way back to the base," Heidi said. "Where is everyone?"

"They're making weapons as far as I can tell. Getting ready to go to war. Against whites. Against strangers. Against atheists. Against everything I am. I convinced them I could be a good spy, so they've spared me but I'm not sure for how long."

Maxine looked unsure of herself, and Heidi wondered if she was a peace offering to show Jira that she could be trusted and how much time that would actually buy her.

"Maybe they'll like me as their token tourist better than you," Heidi suggested and wondered if she was pushing her luck.

"Could be. I don't think anyone here has my back. That's why I volunteered to be in charge of the rations. So, people will have a reason to be nice to me."

"This is a prison, sister," Heidi said. "It's worse. This is a fucking tomb. You and I need to get out of here. Back to the base. They'll let us back in."

"I'm scared," Maxine said. "I've been putting on a brave face but it's just a mask."

"We gals need to stick up for each other. Untie me. We'll run for it. They won't dare go after a pair of witches like us."

Maxine held up Heidi's confiscated knife and studied it, the blade vibrating in her shaking hand. "There was once a bird that flew into my window but I'm the one that drew it there," Maxine said. "With my reflection staring out into the universe with malignance. I was bummed out about this until I realized my daughter was that bird…is that bird. When I saw you, I wanted you to be drawn to my reflection and what you can be."

Heidi took a deep breath and tried to keep her shit together because it was obvious that Maxine was losing hers. "Yes, I'm your baby bird," Heidi said. For a moment, the entire room seemed to shrink and expand again, and her mouth was dry, all the symptoms of drugs but the genesis was her mind unspooling, her unsleeping fucking mind. She tried not to scream. She wanted to get untied more than anything, enough to use a childish tone, "I need you to show me the way."

Heidi smiled as Maxine slid the knife across her bare arm to the rope. She closed her eyes and counted to ten. The rhythm of the blade sawing was like a DJ's beat; it was the theme song of freedom if only she didn't move. She remembered so many nights, pumped up with drugs, dancing in front of customers and ignoring everything but the beat. She was a soap bubble trying not to be popped. She was losing her mind.

Heidi couldn't shake the notion that she was in a dream, to be more accurate, a nightmare. Perhaps the disaster around her might disappear if she were to awaken. But how *woke* were people ever? Even in the best of times? Heidi's eyes fluttered open, and Maxine looked pleased with herself. On the counter, the severed rope hung in strands and several tendrils touched Heidi's bare arms and legs. She fought an irrational urge to leap down and shake the tiny snakes from her. When she did slide to the floor, she needed to steady herself with one hand as she fought against vertigo.

Maxine took the opportunity to slide a fluffy pink band off her wrist and tie it around Heidi's hair, double-knotted into a ponytail. Heidi shuddered at the contact, the breath on her neck, and took the opportunity to reclaim her knife that had been used to cut her free and return it to the scabbard on her belt. She boiled beneath the unwanted human contact but was used to it from the years of lap dances. When Maxine was finished Heidi shot her back a winning smile.

"Thank you," Heidi said, even though she almost said *fuck you*. She noticed Maxine's red hair hung in the same pink ponytail holder. "I'm just like you now."

"Spitting image," Maxine said. "Time to follow mama bird."

Maxine turned her back on Heidi and strolled toward the door like nothing happened, like she hadn't just assaulted and kidnapped her. For a moment, Heidi considered stabbing Maxine to eliminate another threat. No. She refused to succumb to her baser impulses, or she would be lost. Another deep breath. The moment passed. They approached the front door, half-open now as though someone has entered. Maxine looked back coyly, and a knife plunged into her side.

Time slipped again. Christ. Had she done this? Heidi's one good eye traced the knife's hilt to a hand, then to an arm disappearing into a green rain poncho. What Heidi thought had been a display mannequin was actually Jira, in creepy camouflage, watching and waiting in the shadows. He snorted and yanked the blade out. Maxine's face bloomed with incredulity, flushed with an intense, horrible beauty, blood seeping through her fingers pressed to her side to cover the wound.

"This is what you get for crossing me," Jira said.

"Run sweetheart," a voice whispered in Heidi's head, the sound of her mother emerging from the human trash. Instead of trying to stuff down the craziness, she embraced it. *Yes, mama.* She lurched into motion.

Time seemed to hover now. Almost stop. She dodged a frenzied knife thrust by Jira and leapt behind Maxine. As Jira pivoted to lunge at her again, Heidi halted her forward momentum, planted her feet, and shoved Maxine sidelong into him. They tumbled over the display table of ponchos and beachwear, out of sight. A fog seemed to lift now that she could see the light streaming from outside. She yanked open the door and fled out into the sunlight.

Cries behind her transformed into cries on the beach. It was chaos in D-town. To her right, three teenage boys with makeshift clubs were dueling with John and Juan, back-to-back, swinging oars. The fishermen were more ferocious but had a hard time covering the attackers who surrounded them in a triangle. To her left, Heidi recognized Puma, a gigantic man in a red tracksuit, from the stories she'd heard circulating around the island. He took aim with a pistol and fired at two hotel maids rushing out of Thunderdome. Were they the wives of the fishermen? They collapsed in unison. Synchronized dying. A new Olympic sport. The sensory input was too much. Her knees buckled. Her body felt like it was shutting down from too much stress. Too much destruction. Too much inhumanity.

Maxine's scream pierced through the haze, "Run for your life!"

This prompted Puma to turn his attention toward the D-stop just as Jira raced outside, kicking up sand, waving his own pistol. His poncho was slick with blood and the village leader's feral expression shifted to fear.

"Enough!" Heidi cried out. "You should all be ashamed. These are people dying. They had hopes. Dreams. People who love them. Throw down the damn guns."

Jira snarled, fired wildly at her feet, and dived back inside the D-Stop. Puma paused momentarily before pointing his pistol at her. Battle cries continued beside her, and she heard the sounds of weapons clanging on weapons. Grunts. Screams. She held up her hands in surrender but eyed the ocean not fifty feet away. *If she could just make it to the surf.*

Puma's face was crestfallen as he pointed his pistol at Heidi. This hesitation provided cover for several women to race out of Thunderdome, including Margarita, one of the resort maids. Margarita, nearly as large as Puma, saw an opportunity and snuck up behind him, gripping him in a bear hug.

This was all too much for Heidi to handle. The woods or the water? She thought she saw Lilian motioning for her to join her in the brush, but she'd have to run past the devil in the D-stop. She sprinted across the sand and dived into the waves, swimming as fast as she could. More gunshots and yells drifted across the water, and she couldn't make herself look at the carnage. Their nightmares had become reality and their reality had become nightmares. She took a moment to tread water, uncap the go pills, and dry swallowed two to give her enough strength to swim around the cliffs. Her eyes closed and she remembered her swim teacher's voice, one she respected before the creep's hands wandered during instruction, to correct her stroke.

151

She was pretty sure that his was the first hard penis she'd felt pressed against her, in the water, the lesson of the snake continuing with dates, dances, drunken strangers. She laughed and swallowed salt water. She was damn-near dying and all she could think about was penises, and the men who pushed them at her like divining rods looking for treasure.

She did not need men. Maybe that was the lesson of the snake. Rick would not be coming back to save her, or if he did maybe it would be too late. She came out of her fevered remembrances into the dolphin pens next to the scorched docks. She found herself wishing Flo and Jet hadn't abandoned her like her boyfriend, that there was a person she could count on. Even though it was balmy out, mid-day, she shivered as she lay on her foam roller that she sometimes used for yoga back when everything and everyone wasn't trying to kill her. This was just a symptom. Her immune system was under attack, her organs straining to compensate for the lack of REM, the dreamscape of the world killing her bit by bit. But not right now. Not today. She could count on herself, at least.

She put on cargo shorts and one of Rick's button-down shirts from the lockers, nearly as much from muscle memory as anything else, and strapped on her knife and tossed a few bottles of water and MREs into what was formerly her running backpack back when she would jog on Venice Beach. She slung the sniper rifle Rick left with her over her shoulder. *Expect disaster at every moment, yes.* Why else then were the doors to the SEAL base open? It wasn't just the doors leading to the dock. A quick loop around the complex revealed that there was no one in the back kitchen or barracks. The double front doors had been left ajar, just like the back entrance, as an invitation.

She now felt like an intruder in her own home, but this was misguided. She was the guest of honor, although she didn't understand it at first when she craned her head into the living room. Four men sat in chairs, all turned outward away from the TV to face the door. Two were tied up like she had recently been. One was a stranger. One held a handgun. This was not her fucking day.

"Save me," Owen said, tied to a dining room chair next to his assistant Landry who shook his head frantically, straining against his own bonds, and pleading, "Save me instead."

152

Clint sat cross-legged in an easy chair, pistol resting on one knee crossed leisurely over the other, like he was king of the manor. A familiar looking man sat on his left, an overweight guy with a childish face but a wrinkled forehead beneath gray hair, a corncob pipe in his hand, and a leer inhabiting the space between his nose and chin.

"I'm Quinn, this used to be my home, but I've decided to hand it over to my new heir Clint."

"Hail to the conquering hero," Clint said. "We were getting bored. Quinn convinced me that in order to win you have to play."

"Indeed," Quinn giggled.

"They are both fucking high as kites. Get me out of here," Owen said.

"Focus, Heidi. Listen. I'm counting on you," Landry said.

"Don't play coy, princess. We're going to play a game. You decide which one of these assholes lives by killing the other one. Simple choice. Otherwise, I kill them both," Clint said.

Heidi took this threat seriously, knowing Clint had helped that depressed groom Trevor strap a bomb to his chest. Someone was going to die in this living room, and if she weren't careful, it would be her. She would need to be bold and tip the balance in her favor.

Quinn lifted his pipe to Clint's lips and lit it with a long match that he struck against the side of his chair before holding it over the bowl. Clint toked and held smoke in his lungs before coughing loudly. Heidi smelled something familiar, hash most likely, and she remembered the story of how Landry had betrayed Quinn. There was a lot going on here that she didn't understand and wondered how things had devolved since she left the men on the roof.

While the two men passed the pipe back and forth, Heidi strode toward Owen and pulled her knife out of it scabbard. "Thank God," he said, and she remembered him asking her to do him a favor of another kind. She steadied herself and sank the knife into Owen heart with two hands and wiped the blade calmly on his shirt before sawing at Landry's bonds. Clint and Quinn fell out of their chairs and scrambled to their feet, with grunts of surprise and swear words. It took her only a few seconds to cut Landry free and she helped the shaking man to his feet, his circulation probably cut off for some length of time. She probably should feel something close to remorse after killing a man, but she refused to feel sorry for that piece of shit. She was the victim here, and she'd given herself and Landry a fighting chance.

"Jesus Christ, I can't believe you just fucking did that," Clint said. "You are stone cold, baby."

"I wish you'd made a different decision," Quinn said. "Landry will betray you. Wait and see. All you've done is give yourself a head start. We're going to hunt you down and then we're going to smoke your asses."

"Get it, that's a double entendre," Clint said. "Or maybe a pun. Either way, you're a dead man and woman walking."

"You mean running," Heidi said. She half pushed, half-pulled Landry to keep pace with her as she raced around the corner and out the front door. The caretaker was disheveled and probably in shock, but he kept up with her as they hit the gates and ran like their lives depended on it. She slid the rifle off her shoulder and held it like a divining rod. *It would show her blood, yes.* The clouds looked like monsters in the sky, overcast and threatening rain. Heidi wiped her eyes and realized her fingers were dripping with blood, her new mascara, her fucking war paint, her sins staining her flesh for the world to see.

CHAPTER 21

Russell Copeland

NO DEATHS. AT LEAST, NOT yet. The food poisoning in the kitchen had made the remaining bridesmaids throw up, with a bad case of the shakes, all except for Kara who reluctantly set them up poolside and provided them with water and wet towels to help keep them from overheating. Marley had refused to help any of them, and Russell couldn't blame him for being not so secretly pleased with what had taken place. The resort owner missed Daniela but was too selfish at his core to have really loved her. He hadn't given enough of himself and now here he was providing a shoulder to lean on to the women who had killed her. His whole moral center was leaking and in the absence of certainty he played caretaker, the man focused on the details. Marley stood on the periphery, holding his grandfather's cricket bat and staring out at the burnt-out husk of Cava.

Russell recognized how much Marley was hoping to please his father but was unable to do so. This had been the case with his own father as well. He was the idiot son without vision who scheduled the ice trucks and made sure the wheels kept spinning. *My secretary* is how the old man introduced him to his friends at Harkins, a private gentleman's club that met in spots around the city for brandy and to hunt whatever game was in season. Russell

155

had no love of guns. His father had taught him how to shoot but was pissed when he refused his right of manhood. No buck on the hunt for his thirteenth birthday. No reason for Russell to ever be invited back to join him at the club, not even as an adult, no matter how often he hinted at it.

His father had hated how much he wanted his approval. Russell suspected that Gibraltar might be a similar kind of asshole. The kid needed a distraction and, luckily, his addictive personality supplied one. He'd stashed away a bottle of rum in his satchel, or what his father would have called a man purse, but he needed a cigarette. And those were now in short supply.

"Let's go back into Cava and see if we can snag me some smokes. If anyone can find cigs there, you can," Russell said.

Marley didn't say anything but nodded in response. Doing anything, even busywork, was better for the kid than waiting around for the next tragedy. Russell had started rifling through the cabanas of his guests that had departed this world and had found the most success in the comped room of the Boy Georges. He'd found a couple packs of Marlboro reds that he'd already burned his way through. It was shocking how much more quickly you sucked down smokes when you didn't sleep and were stressed all the time. He missed the Georges. The easygoing brother/sister tandem might have helped stop some of these moonstruck morons running amuck.

They crossed the beach to Cava gingerly. They were both still sore from carrying Daniela, even though neither would admit it. The landscape had transformed from a typical postcard vista with sugary sand and palm trees to an apocalyptic dayscape. The beach extended far into the distance with disruption to the tides, exposing coral now bleached, the bones of the earth poking skyward, the wreck of the reef symptomatic of the destruction inside all of them.

Russell followed Marley through the charred ruins of Cava to the back stairwell, the basement all that remained of the bar. The booze had already been pilfered by the groomsmen, but he hoped that they'd left cigarettes undisturbed. He had enough of a private stash of liquor in his own room to last awhile, choosing now to sneak drinks alone so that others wouldn't ask to join him. He was in survival mode but instead of food and water, his necessities began and ended with nicotine and alcohol. At the bottom of the steps, Marley wandered over to the bookshelf by a window covered in dirt. The kid muttered to himself and leafed through a few thin volumes of poetry. Russell didn't recognize the names on the spines: Garcia, Young, Chang, Corral, Kasischke, Berry. His own taste in books gravitated toward mysteries, a pursuit that had not prepared him well enough for the mystery of why they were all dying.

He laughed at his own joke and realized he hadn't been speaking. He rummaged through boxes of napkins and toilet paper, mixers and tumblers. He was losing himself in himself, crawling inside his memories so that he wouldn't fall to the fluttering periphery and face the ghost of the father he was sure had followed him everywhere he went. At least it wasn't Daniela, or was it? A woman's foot slipped out from beneath a tarp and Russell yelped.

The wrinkled black covering flew in the air like a ghost from some alternative negative zone universe. Marley turned at the sound and fell backward, pulling his books down on him. Russell backed away and sat on an empty beer case and it collapsed beneath him. Beneath the tarp emerged Heidi, the dolphin caretaker, and Landry, the SEAL base custodian. The young woman looked like she was in shock and muttered, "I'm in the human trash," but that made no sense. Landry gripped what looked like a military sniper rifle, but the safety was on. Russell's father at least had prepared him for this moment.

"Hey guys, how are you?" Russell asked.

"We're all going to die. What do you think?" Heidi asked.

Marley cocked his arm as though to launch a tome of poetry, then reconsidered seeing the rifle wagging back and forth between himself and Russell. "Why did you leave the SEAL base? Isn't it the safest place on the entire caye?" the kid asked.

"Not when there's a lunatic with the keys to the arsenal around like it's *The Island of Dr. Moreau*," Landry said.

"Jesus," Marley said.

"Why is that bad?" Russell asked.

"He's hunting humans," Marley explained.

"THEY are hunting humans. That horrible man Quinn appeared, and it didn't take him long to poison that recruit's mind. Clint has lost it."

"I'm pretty sure he helped Trevor to strap that explosive vest on himself," Heidi said. "He's dangerous. Otherwise, I wouldn't have…"

The woman's hands shook, and he could see that she was having a hard time controlling herself: body, mind, spirit. They were all being pushed past their boundaries, borders, and abilities. But that was what SEAL training was about, and their instructors were supposed to stay on mission no matter what obstacles they faced.

"What about Rick?" Russell asked.

"The guy disappeared on us," Landry said.

"They always leave me. Except for the ones in the trash," Heidi said. "They never leave."

It was obvious that Heidi had gone through some trauma and Landry wasn't much better. First things first. "Do you mind not pointing that rifle at us?" Russell asked. His voice was calm, at least he imagined it was, but a wave of anxiety threatened to capsize him. If he weren't already sitting on his ass he'd need to as the tiny basement room spun.

"Sure thing, mate." Landry lowered the rifle and looked around uncomfortably.

"I think we should go talk to my father," Marley said.

"Are you sure that's a good idea?" Russell asked. He reached a hand back on the cardboard box to lift himself and it slid inside. Eureka. He yanked out a half-crushed carton of Camels, with several packs rattling inside of it. He smiled and pocketed them before standing. Minor victory this, but a victory all the same.

"Some of us are wrecking each other but Puma is a killer," Marley said. "So is my father. They're not soldiers taught to have honor. They're vicious, unscrupulous, and it's better to be kissing the ring than kissing the dirt."

Daniela's death had affected the kid. He was more jaded, but sure of himself, and looking through the lens of adulthood. Tragedy had brought out the best in him and Gibraltar wasn't around to notice. Russell's own father had been an imposing figure who excelled at making others kiss his ass until his own son betrayed him and sold his kingdom to build another. And what a failure Russell had been. Even though he'd sweated the details he'd lost his fiefdom to a Hollywood director and a local politician. People were dying at his resort in increasing frequency and, to make matters worse, he found himself caring less about anyone's survival other than his own. He was a coward, a living coward, and he planned to stay that way.

"I think you should listen to the kid. I am," he said.

"Marley, you're in charge then. Lead the way," Heidi said, holding out her hand and accepting a cigarette from Russell who took the time to open a pack and light them both up. They both took a moment to fill their lungs with smoke and Russell managed not to cough on his way up the stairs even though he was winded, even though he was more tired than he'd ever been before in his life. He stood at the top of the landing and heard his father calling for help below, like he must have done after breaking his hip until his parched throat stopped working. Dad's final days must have been torture and Russell was responsible, his inaction to check on the old man bordering on the criminal.

Russell whistled a pop tune that had been popular before he boarded the plane to Belize and was grateful that Marley had chosen the dock path back to the resort instead of the direct route where Kara's bridesmaids and relatives lay writhing from the poison. The sun was starting its descent into the water, and he made the mistake of looking it in the eye. Spots danced and he saw the waves curl up like eyelashes in the distance, a tidal wave that would swallow them all. Perhaps it was another nuclear explosion or else God finally putting them all out of their misery. He stopped and dropped in the sand, helpless and drawing in smoke, closing his eyes and wishing he'd been a better man.

"That must be some cigarette," Heidi said.

Russell opened his lids and there was no giant wave heading toward them just his mind unraveling. "You don't even want to know what I just saw."

"Trade you," Heidi said, and he found himself scared of her and for her.

He got to his feet and hurried to catch up with Marley and Landry, Heidi keeping pace. She flipped her butt into the sand before hitting the cobblestone walkway, but Russell fought the urge to litter. If they did not follow the niceties nothing would keep them from acting like savages, more than they were already. He pinched the end of the cigarette and pocketed the filter. Landry and Marley were waiting for them, and the kid convinced the mansion caretaker that it was better to leave the rifle behind. Russell held out his hands and deposited it in a stand of flotation devices situated next to the cobblestone path leading to the pool.

They found Gibraltar holding court at the ping pong table gripping a paddle and occasionally swatting Kara on the behind. She was bent over the table, palms flat, her face flush and obviously enjoying the *game*. This didn't mean that Marley's father wasn't paying attention. Before they made it halfway down the path, Gibraltar reached down and expertly pointed the hunting rifle at them.

"I have two people seeking refuge from the mansion. Someone there has gone nuts," Marley said. "They're dangerous."

"Everyone is nuts and dangerous," Gibraltar said.

"You have no idea," Puma said, stepping out from behind a palm tree, his hand gripping a pistol, his red tracksuit stained with blood.

The parents of the boys with biblical names burst out of a cabana and ran up to Puma. They must have been watching the courtyard from a distance. Russell couldn't hear what they said only that Puma shrugged and the couple ran off into the jungle on the path he'd just taken. He hoped they would find the boys alive but feared the worst.

"Puma, what do you think we should do about these intruders?" Gibraltar asked.

"I only have two bullets left." Puma trudged toward them like he was carrying the weight of the world on his shoulders.

"And there are two of them," Kara said, standing up and rubbing her bottom so that everyone looked at her, trying to be the center of attention, even now.

"I just killed a woman who looked just like my mother," Puma said. "And those boys you sent along with me got wrecked. Everyone got wrecked."

"You did your job, my friend," Gibraltar said.

"Don't you see that these things don't go together? *Job. Friend.* I killed people who didn't deserve it. Everyone you asked me to take care of before this deserved it," Puma said.

"This conversation doesn't sound like it involves us," Heidi said, starting to back away.

"No one fucking move," Puma said, pointing his pistol at Heidi, then Landry.

Kara laughed and Russell couldn't help himself. He took several paces forward and slapped her. Hard. She only laughed harder.

"Puma, you are family. Please. Let's talk about this. You're OK. I knew you would be," Gibraltar said.

"I'm not OK. I see how you treat family. You kill family. You killed me. Everything in me that matters."

Puma aimed at the paddle Gibraltar was holding and pulled the trigger. The wooden shaft exploded, and it started raining splinters. A red hole appeared in Gibraltar's shirt, and he collapsed, his rifle clacking to the ground. Russell looked to make sure he wasn't bleeding from the shards as Marley rushed over to this father. The kid slid his leg under his father's head, but his eyes were glassy. He was gone.

"One bullet left. Who deserves to die? The son?" Puma pointed the pistol at Marley who fought to extricate himself from his father's body, then at Kara. "Or the witch? Or how about the resort owner who let everyone take over?"

"Yes, please, shoot me," Russell said. "Maybe this is my one shot at redemption." And he realized it was a pun, probably the last of his life.

"This choice is the easiest one I'll ever make." Puma shoved the pistol under his jaw and pulled the trigger. Blood sprayed over them, and they were all specked with blood, from head to toe. Puma fell headfirst and everything was chaos. Heidi leaned down and pulled Marley to his feet, while Landry ran toward the rifle that Gibraltar had dropped.

Kara was quicker. She picked it up and pointed it at them, one at a time, the lust in her eyes dancing with a combination of anger and happiness. "This is my joint now, Russell. Get out of here, bitches, before I lose my temper."

She didn't have to say this twice. They were all arms and legs as they scrambled away toward the pool. Heidi paused to get the sniper rifle and didn't listen as Kara yelled at her to drop it. Marley raced to the poolside bar and snagged his cricket bat. The foursome ignored the groaning women on lounge chairs and rushed headlong into the jungle, nothing in the wild as scary as what they faced here, or anywhere else humans resided on the island.

"You better run," Kara yelled behind them, and they obliged.

CHAPTER 22

Russell Copeland

THE CHURCH. MARLEY WAS THE first to suggest this destination as a sanctuary. They needed a place to regroup, and Russell didn't have a better idea. Apparently, their impromptu foursome was encircled by the remains of the island's inhabitants armed with guns, clubs, and ill intent. The confines of the jungle, compared to the alternatives, felt like the equivalent of hiding under a bed or nestling in the back of a closet when hiding from monsters. Safe, but perhaps the safety was an illusion.

"Don't worry. I am a pixie. I am holding the light," Heidi said.

Russell wasn't sure what that meant in the blooming dusk, only that the path zigzagging through the brush was unfamiliar and that they had become children again with full access to skittish imaginations and an easily accessible dreamscape. And children had become adults. Marley led the way now with conviction, his father's death a catalyst for him to step up and fill the void of leadership. They had strayed off the paths Russell knew, however, and he worried that they were going in circles.

"I know where I'm going," Marley said as though reading Russell's thoughts before placating his fears. "We'll get our bearings at the twisted tree."

Russell's interactions with Quinn on the phone during their negotiations for the resort had been a monotonous affair, the men shepherded by lawyers through paperwork, their interactions minimal. At the end of their final teleconference, Quinn spoke of the heart of the island, a *twisted tree* rumored to change locations depending on the emotional wellbeing of the caye's residents. A misnomer. As it was not one tree but two married by twisting trunks and limbs together in a single looming mass that thrust skyward as a single entity above the level of its neighbors.

Marley was as good as his word. They eventually arrived at the twisted tree on a path that had nearly disappeared. Light ebbed. Bird chirps ceased. A scratching sound drifted from inside the conjoined trunk splayed open from the torque of the trees over time. Inside was a tiny space, an altar the locals sometimes used for religious totems and jewelry that would be stolen by birds and woven in nests throughout the island.

"I'm a pixie," Heidi repeated, clicking on a flashlight and pointing the beam inside the tree trunk. None of them could process what had been left on the altar, a man with three jagged branches jutting out of his chest. It was a nightmare come to life. This visage couldn't be real, only that it was. It was the artist Enrique, impaled, and his eyes danced with creative energy.

"Father, son, and holy ghost. The trinity is now inside me. Only I never really believed before now," Enrique said.

He dipped the fingers of each hand into his wounds, and he stretched out his arms on either side. Two self-portraits were painted on the interior of the tree. These murals were alike in every way, except that the figure on the left had an elongated goatee and horns, and the man on the right had angel wings. He added flames with blood on both sides, to the halo and to cloven feet. This was the most beautiful thing Russell had ever seen.

"We need to get him out of there," Marley said.

"We can't. He'll bleed out," Heidi said.

"Jesus, who did this?" Landry asked.

"He's your savior and mine," Enrique said. "Jira said my sacrifice wouldn't be in vain."

Heidi bent down, examining the wounds before clasping her hands together as though in prayer. A silhouette crashed through the brush, and they all jumped backwards. The creature was all arms and legs, gripping a metal canister, arm cocked to throw.

"Bomb," Landry yelled, and they all dove into the brush, clearing a path to the tree trunk. The silhouette stepped into the flashlight beam and the intruder coalesced there, an otherworldly creature now in human form. It was Lilian, holding a canteen, her hands streaked with blood, her face flushed and her eyes darting like some demonic doll.

"Get away from him!" Lilian yelled. "You're all to blame. You've brought ruin to Devil's Caye."

"Jira did this? He killed my grandfather, too," Marley said.

"This is my masterpiece," Enrique said.

"This is madness," Russell said, certain that they would all be pulled into the twisted tree if they stayed long enough.

"I'm a pixie." Heidi pointed her flashlight back at Enrique and Lilian took the opportunity to hold the bottle to his lips. The artist kept drawing with blood, seemingly immune to pain or his impending demise. "Jira made me into a vessel for his seed when I was a boy. He told me that he and I were a twisted tree, and that I deserve to die for my wickedness."

"No, you don't," Marley said.

"We're all dying," Lilian barked. "The only thing left is now how we choose to die. I'm staying here with my man. You can all go to hell for all I care."

Lilian turned her back on them and Russell pleaded with Marley for them to go. He did this with his eyes. Then it dawned on him that he had not used his words. The simplest things were now beyond him, but the kid seemed to get the message.

"Follow me," Marley said and there wasn't a single voice of dissent. Day had transitioned to dusk, and the woods creaked with something that wasn't wind or creatures. It was ghosts, all of their ghosts, or they were the ghosts, and they were haunting the world of spirits. Russell could feel his father's breath on his neck, and he expected the belt would be next, the sting of lashes. After getting beaten, he remembered getting locked in the basement and his father snapping the light off. The punishment was worse than anything else because of his fear of the dark, his imagination opening an abyss that his mother would have kept him from sliding into, the light in the fridge, the beer in the basement, the beginning of his addiction. His prison when his father was pissed at him. Russell would get his revenge, though. It was the same basement his father died in.

It was the blind leading the blind, the darkness emanating from inside them and flowing through the woods. The battered moon either had not risen or was hiding from them. Like small children in a fairy tale, they gripped hands and tried not to get lost, but this was impossible because they were beyond all boundaries. Marley was their beacon, his curly black hair visible from Heidi's flashlight. And true to his word, they found shelter at the abandoned church.

Russell came out of his trance at Daniela's grave and the gravity of their situation came into focus. They were still alive while many others were not. Heidi reached into her backpack and handed them all go pills to help them gather their senses. Any self-control or guardrails that had come from Russell's sobriety had long since vanished, along with all of their dreams. Literally and figuratively.

They approached the church, pushing open the door and settling into the ramshackle pews, mildewed and worn from the elements and neglect. Fragments of stained glass had transformed nearly back to sand after so many years of squatters hanging out in the ruins. The altar was bare—everything of value had been stripped away years before. There had been no church services here in a generation and the spiritual center of the island had shifted to Thunderdome. The inside smelled like mildew and flowers, the perfume from the wildflowers surrounding the building.

Heidi pulled out a packet of military glow sticks, and did a short circuit, snapping a half dozen open and casting them all in an eerie green glow. She tossed each of them an MRE from her stash and they scarfed the meals, not even stopping to hydrate the meat packets. Russell didn't even remember his last meal. Between the energy from their impromptu dinner and the charge from the amphetamine capsule, he felt sharper than he had in days. He almost felt safe surrounded by stone and walled off from the kaleidoscope of horror they'd witnessed over the past few days.

With two glow sticks crisscrossed in the aisle like campfire embers they sat around in a circle sharing stories of happiness and heartache, the confessions in that place borne from the knowledge that they might not survive more than a few hours or days, that they all had regrets and walls that needed to be mended or torn down. Marley and Heidi bonded over mothers who were distant in every way possible. Russell could sense some deeper pain in Landry and, even though they'd barely shared more than a few niceties of drinks at the Cava Bar, he felt as though he could read the caretaker like a book.

"I killed a man, my father," Russell said.

"I killed a boy, and he never became a man," Landry admitted.

"He fell down the stairs and he died alone, knowing that I must have known something was wrong but did nothing to save him," Russell said.

"Quinn was with me the day of the accident. I worked for him as much for access to drugs as anything. I was a wild kid traveling the Caribbean after my parents died, working odd jobs, and Quinn took me on as his driver and assistant of sorts. We ended up here when he got in trouble in Costa Rica and was looking to become legit."

"Sounds like my family," Marley said.

"I was driving his speedboat with some of his high roller gambling buddies in the earlier hours of the morning, higher than the moon. I ended up hitting Luis, one of the kids in D-town just around dawn. I have no idea why he was out in the water that early. We pulled him into the boat and took him back to the mansion. We tried everything to bring him back. We ended up stuffing him in a duffle bag and burying him outside this church. I figured the best place to get rid of a body was in a graveyard."

"Luis is here?" Heidi asked.

"Yes, in an unmarked grave. And that's the worst part. His parents thought he drowned. His mother went crazy and killed herself. Her father went crazy, too. In his own way. His father is Jira. And I'm responsible for him being a lunatic."

"No one is responsible for anyone else," Russell said.

"I wish that were so. Quinn blackmailed me for what I'd done, and he turned me into a ghost of a man. His obedient servant in an island prison who eventually would turn the tables and get his revenge. But by then my life was over. It IS over," Landry said.

"All our lives are over," Marley said, and gallows humor won out, at least for the moment, as they laughed until they were gassed.

"I'm not a pixie," Heidi said, and they laughed some more.

"I've always hated the sunrise because of what I did but I want to watch this one," Landry said. "See you later, mates."

Landry lifted himself off the pew and wandered outside. Another day awaited them if they were brave enough to face it. Heidi pulled out a bottle and passed two pills to each of them. "Last ones," she said.

Russell swallowed his with a gulp of water, passing the plastic bottle to Marley who did the same. They were at the end of the rations Heidi had packed and back to facing the grim realities of securing more.

"It's funny, the world is ending and I'm feeling guilty about littering. No trash cans here. Not that anyone can see," Heidi said, stuffing the empty pill bottle in her front pocket with quivering hands.

"I'm all messed up. I'm alternating between being too hot and too cold. There's a ringing in my ears now," Marley said.

"We're like cars whose engine has been running without oil. Eventually we'll blow a gasket," Russell said, his father's definition of being a man included being able to change your own oil. He refused to do this as an adult out of spite more than anything, but he did take good care of his cars if not his family.

"I'm feeling claustrophobic in here," Heidi said. "My mother would have loved this church. She's telling me so. I'm fucking losing it."

Heidi packed up her backpack and slid it on before following Landry out the door. Russell and Marley didn't know what to say, the ultimate odd couple, the kind only a true shit show like this could have brought together. They were each lost in their own memories until a woman's scream jolted them back into the world. Marley gripped his cricket bat and raced toward the door. It was then that Russell noticed the sniper rifle. He picked it up with trembling hands and clicked off the safety, before stumbling headlong toward whatever horrors awaited him outside.

Chapter 23

Heidi Radar

HEIDI SHRIEKED WHEN SHE SAW the rifle. The barrel was pointed at her as soon as she rounded the corner. The rifle belonged to Clint Jenkins, his red freckles not yet visible in the early morning hours but his goatee was even more goat-like, more animalistic. Next to him Quinn was poking and prodding at Landry with his hands held above his head and a look of tired resignation. Not fear. Not even when Quinn pulled a container of lighter fluid out of his satchel and doused Landry a squeeze at a time, a body part at a time. What new hell was this?

This would, of course, be a good time for Rick to appear, but she had come to the realization that he was on his own path now, and it was unlikely to cross hers, if indeed he was still alive. She hoped Rick was safer on the mainland than they were on Devil's Caye. It was time to be realistic. She refused to retreat back into some fantasy of becoming a legendary beast or mythic figure. Heidi Radar was a flawed woman, who wanted to keep living at nearly any cost. She could make this identity work for her if she were smart and brave enough.

"Landry, did you really think I wouldn't get my revenge?" Quinn asked. "I'm going to smoke you."

Marley raced around the corner, cricket bat held like a sword. Clint spun and pointed the rifle muzzle at the kid, who slid to a stop and settled into a strange stance. Mercifully, Russell didn't join the scene. She hoped the resort owner would recognize the danger and set up somewhere out of view with the rife. There was a round in the chamber and she hoped he knew how to handle a gun.

Between Quinn's dilapidated monk's robe, Clint's ripped SEAL uniform, Landry's wrinkled pinstripe dress pants and vest, Marley's blood-splattered cricket bat, and her white-trash shorts and bikini top they were like some apocalypse island version of *The Village People.*

"Hey, do you guys get it? We're all in costume," Heidi said. "Sailor. Monk. Butler. Cricketeer. Stripper. Like a band. I've got an idea, let's sing YMCA." Heidi began belting out the song but didn't know why she broke into dance, old habits from stripping perhaps when she lip-synced her favorite songs. Her voice was never good, but she wasn't terribly off-key either. That lunatic Quinn stopped spritzing Landry for a second, mouth open.

"Yes, just like the motherfucking Village People," Quinn said and joined in the haphazard dance, robes flying up and revealing nothing underneath.

"Jesus, too bad the internet is toast. This would make a great video to post," Clint said.

Even Marley couldn't help but break a smile, and he used the opportunity to edge closer to Heidi instead of running off into the brush. She made it through the first chorus of the song before Clint shot his rifle in the air. A couple of birds flew off from the boughs of a nearby tree while she and Quinn paused mid-dance step.

"Heidi, if I'm going to rule this place, I can't get rid of everyone," Quinn said. "I'll let you entertain me and if you're nice we can keep the kid around to serve me back at the mansion."

"I'd be glad to help you, too, sir," Landry said in a subservient tone, eyes down.

"Bollocks, you're a big old wanker. Quinn told me how you betrayed him, mate," Clint said with a faux-British accent. "And you've never liked me much anyway."

"Maybe I just need to get to know you as the leader you've become

170

instead of a trainee."

"Landry, my man, don't be a suck-up. You've burned too many bridges," Quinn said, dropping the now-empty can of lighter fluid into a patch of orange wildflowers and pulling his lighter out from behind his ear like a long-practiced magic trick from a man with infinite time and madness.

"Fair enough," Landry said. "Let me go and you'll never see me again."

"You've won, Clint. You've proven that you're the man. Rick couldn't protect me or any of us. It's obvious you can. Let Landry go. He's no threat," Heidi pleaded.

She was appealing to the trainee's ego and trying to buy time. Russell had either decided to set up for a shot or to desert them. Either way, she needed to do everything she could to give them all a fighting chance. That weirdo Quinn really looked like he wanted to *smoke* them all, whatever that meant.

Clint's right ear disappeared as a bullet ricocheted behind him and blood sprayed in every direction. "Dammit," he yelled, holding a hand to the side of his head where his ear had been.

Heidi turned her head, afraid to move, and saw Russell taking cover behind a headstone, bullets flying around him as Clint returned fire. The resort owner kept his head down, the sniper rifle set into his shoulder with hopefully a few more rounds loaded. On automatic fire, it only took a few seconds for Clint's rifle to empty itself.

Like Heidi, Quinn and Landry were frozen in place, hoping to avoid the gunfire. Not Marley—the kid rushed toward Clint, cricket bat over his head, shrieking like a crazy person. Hell, they were all crazy people at this point.

"Don't let him reload," Russell yelled, jumping to his feet and fumbling with the sniper rifle.

Many things happened at once and everything slowed to half-speed or else this was just another hallucination from not sleeping. Heidi pulled out her knife at the same time Clint reached for his extra clip. Quinn lit his lighter and Landry turned to flee. With Marley practically on top of him, Clint was forced to drop his extra clip to hold his rifle out in front of him with both hands like a staff. Heidi finally got her legs to move, and she stumbled forward to try to help Marley. Quinn lit his lighter and threw it. The moment the flame hit Landry's kerosene-soaked vest he went up in flames.

This was not happening...only it was. Landry screamed louder than seemed humanly possible. Marley's bat cracked against the stock of Clint's rife. Russell scuttled sideways to get an angle to shoot, causing him to stumble on tree roots. Quinn smiled at the conflagration he'd caused, the human torch formerly known as Landry. This tiredness, this failure of the mind and body, this calamity outwardly focusing their worst flaws, made Heidi weak in the knees. She would not, could not, allow herself to tumble, to roll into a ball, to lose herself in herself.

Marley stepped back to avoid the butt of the rifle narrowly missing his face and swung the cricket bat wildly. "Hey," she cried and feinted toward Clint with the knife but made sure to step away from the arcing barrel whooshing just past her chest. In the periphery she saw Quinn race past with a flaming human backpack, Landry screaming in agony. Clint, with a shocked expression, lowered his guard and Marley swung the blade of the bat into his midriff, driving the sailor backwards. Russell barely managed to dodge Quinn and Landry, both howling and on fire, crashing into the brush and flailing like a multi-armed, multi-legged creature.

Russell fired and Clint jerked sideways, bleeding from the shoulder. He launched an impressive string of obscenities and leapt backward to dodge a knife thrust and another swing of the bat. He turned and sprinted away from the church, probably back to the armory to find bigger and badder weapons to blow them all away. The threesome shouted in joy, in relief, in being alive. They'd faced a trained killer, an elite special-forces operative, and sent him running with his tail between his legs.

They came together in a group hug, each of them holding each other up and clinging to exhaustion, until Marley cried out, "Landry."

"Stay here," Russell insisted.

The resort owner hurried to a stand of trees that had caught fire at the base and saw the lifeless smoldering mass that had settled between two trunks. Heidi turned away so that she wouldn't see the semi-human shapes there. Landry and Quinn were both gone, their animosity finally running its course and setting themselves and the jungle on fire.

"There's no place safe on this island," Russell said.

Heidi nodded and spun around, deep in thought. "True that. We have nothing but bad choices here."

"That's why we're going to leave," Marley said. "I know where Quinn must have left his boat."

Marley led them quickly back inside the church to pick up a couple of water bottles they'd left and by the time they emerged the brush fire had jumped to the treetops. It wouldn't be long before the entire jungle was ablaze. It hadn't rained in days, not since the thunderstorm that had wrecked D-town. Monkeys and birds screeched their alarms and Marley drove them eastward, in the opposite direction that Clint took. This, at least, calmed Heidi's nerves slightly. It had now been a week since the moon had been hit and that's all it had taken to tear the island apart.

She staggered and almost fell trying to keep up, her limbs tingling and back locking up. The effect of the go pills kicked in along with the adrenaline of escaping being burnt to a crisp. She didn't recognize the terrain this far away from the base but gained confidence as she saw the cliffs rise above the treetops.

Marley was muttering to himself as the winding trails became smaller and more numerous. It was a maze of dirt paths that he navigated with twists and turns into underbrush that had grown the further away they'd roamed from the island's inhabitants. It was the closest she'd come to seeing what the caye interior would have looked like if humans had never come to infest it with machetes, flames, and hatred. Perhaps they would be swallowed alive by the foliage before being burned to a crisp. She almost lost hope until a cliff wall loomed and they all gathered a last surge of energy.

Behind them smoke plumed and the wind pushed the fire closer. Heidi coughed and she realized it was out of fear, her body on its last legs. Weird how she thought of herself as a vessel containing herself. *Maybe that's God*, suggested her mother. She felt the heat intensify behind her and she whistled as she ran, a human teakettle. They made their way to the base of the cliff. There yawned five fissures, each narrow and twice the height of a human. These were the entrances to the labyrinth of caves that all of them had been warned about.

"The claw," Marley said, and here was yet another island superstition,

173

that the hand of God had opened these caves to test only the faithful among them. "Three of the entrances are dead ends, and two lead to the beach, one higher up on an overlook and one that opens onto the sand."

"You've explored them, right?" Russell asked.

"No, but Daniela explained the passages to me."

"Jesus, kid, I'm tripping out way too much to lose myself in a maze."

"Heidi, would you please stop whistling?" Marley asked. "I'm trying to think."

Get the glow sticks out, her father's voice commanded, and Heidi pulled out three orange plastic tubes, one for each of them, and snapped them in her hands.

They each took one of the sticks, and they seemed hardly bright enough to see more than a few feet ahead. Even though Heidi had stopped pursing her lips, the caves continued to whistle from the wind whipping through the entrances. Since they'd stopped to ponder their path, the smoke had now caught up to them. Heidi felt a furnace breathing into her ears. Marley closed his eyes and recited what sounded like a poem under his breath. "The middle finger of God," the kid said. A bullet ricocheted inches from his head and laughter rose out of the gray plumes.

Marley opened his eyes and plunged into the middle cavern with Russell on his heels and Heidi a few steps behind. It was dangerous running into darkness, and she immediately scraped her left arm on the entrance. She followed the orange glow bouncing ahead of her and when she lost sight of it, saw a second one. Her right shin hit an outcropping and she stomped her leg in pain. The caves smelled damp and her left tennis shoe splashed in a puddle. *Hope you'll like my cave swim lessons*, her former high school swimming instructor said. She hissed angrily and heard what sounded like laughter behind her. Heidi lost the orange glow ahead and came up to a fork, not sure which one to take. She thought she heard voices on the left and plunged that way and then took another fork on the right as a gunshot echoed behind her.

Heidi coughed on smoke that somehow had made its way this far in and glanced backwards to see if she'd lost her pursuer. By the time she turned back around she saw the jagged wall too late, smacking her forehead and stumbling back on her ass. She rubbed her temples and lay backwards to try to clear her head. There would be none of that. *Figures you'd get on your back for us like the slut that you are.* She felt her human trash spilling out from the crack in her skull. Heidi wanted to scream for help but couldn't chance it. She struggled to try to right herself, fighting against all of her fears at once.

Chapter 24

Marley Vega

MARLEY REFUSED TO TURN BACK in the dark passages to see what followed. Nothing was going to slow him down. Chased by fire and a lunatic with a gun in a cavern that housed bats that would claw him to the bone, or at least that was what he imagined, he didn't stop until he saw the light opening out onto Angel Beach. He would not die below ground like he'd almost done in the basement of Cava, the fire behind him replacing the other in his memory. If there was any place to escape this devil of a caye that had chewed up his family, this was where he needed to be. He never felt more certain of anything before in his life. Marley bruised and scraped his arms and legs bouncing off walls, but his gamble paid off—he accelerated toward a blue fissure. Here sky and water grew larger as he stumbled outside onto stone then sand. A powerboat was anchored offshore between two reefs and even from here he could see the keys in the ignition.

He was burning up now, in a waking fever that seemingly would never end. On his race through the twisting passages, he could swear that he saw creatures fluttering in the caves, perhaps ghosts. He was convinced that Rex had been watching over him. Maybe his father, too. Perhaps he rated as important after death in a way he hadn't when Gibraltar was alive.

176

What about his friends? He was relieved when Russell finally stumbled out into the sunlight and collapsed on the sand beside him. They both looked toward the entrance, and it was then that Marley noticed the red spot soaking Russell's shirt.

"You've been shot," Marley said.

"Never mind that. Heidi's missing."

Marley gripped his cricket bat so hard that he thought it might explode in his hand. He was exhausted and afraid, more than he'd ever experienced in his young life. "I'll go in," Marley said, and he willed himself to head back into the darkness, but his body didn't respond. His knees shook. His heart pounded.

"Nonsense. I'm the one who lost her. I'll find her. You make sure that boat is ready to go. I'm sick of Devil's Caye."

"You mean Copeland Caye," Marley said.

"Oh, what could have been," Russell said.

Russell rose and grabbed two hands of sand, slapping his palms together as though it were chalk like one of the famous basketball players used to do before the start of games. Was that guy still alive? Were any of the icons and villains in the newspapers still kicking or had they all regressed to a state of internal combustion? Without their dreams to pull them from themselves, people had transformed into the basest of emotions, the ones the bible had warned about, the reptilian center of the brain back in charge. There had to be something more. There was love in them all, too, the harder path to be part of something larger than yourself.

"You really thought that you could leave me?" a voice called out from the overhang twenty feet up the cliff.

Jira, shirtless and with shoulder-length hair fluttering in the breeze, stared down and pointed a pistol at Marley, the same smug grin he'd had the night he killed Rex, only his eyes were crazier, his expression more manic, the green devil tattoo dancing on his arm. Then Marley realized that Jira was shaking, the same way they had all been the last few days. Their bodies barely in control.

"I'm glad you're here. I wanted to ask you why you want me dead?" Marley asked.

"You misunderstand. I want you to stay with me. To stay with God."

Marley looked down and noticed that Russell had dropped the sniper rifle in the sand. The night before, the resort owner had explained how his father had shown him how to shoot, something Gibraltar had never done with him. Marley would certainly be shot before he could snag the rifle and it was a half-dozen steps to get back into the cavern or to a small stand of palm trees ringing the cove.

"You're wrong. God is one of the first invaders of this island, this country."

"My son was not a believer and he died, for real. No heaven. No way to see him again. Marley, if I can absolve you of your sins, you'll live forever," Jira said.

"You're wrong. I can feel the spirit of my Grandpapi everywhere and he believed in many things, but not Jesus. Not the Holy Ghost. He told me that this fairy tale was used to keep brown folks like us enslaved. Jira, it's not too late for me to help you, perhaps."

"Said the little devil on Angel Beach," Jira said. "Of course, my faith would be tested here of all places. And I will be worthy of this life and the next one."

Marley heard a scrambling inside the cave and lifted his hands, hopefully to warn his companions. "You've got me. I'm your prisoner."

Russell emerged with Heidi leaning on his shoulder. She looked pale and barely able to carry her own weight, blood trickling from both knees and elbows. The red spot on Russell's shirt had now spread onto his back and stomach.

"I lost the trash in there. The human trash. I set them free. I'm free," Heidi babbled.

"So, the demons have all left you, slut. Good to hear. I can save all of your souls."

Heidi and Russell turned to look up and they groaned at the same time. They'd come so far but it didn't seem like it would be enough.

"I know what happened to Luis," Russell said.

"Shut up! You have no right to say his name," Jira said, re-aiming his pistol at Russell.

178

"Luis didn't drown. If you want to know what happened to him drop the gun and come down here. I'll share everything I know," Russell said.

"You lie. You all deserve to join Luis in the afterlife."

"Someone on this island killed him. Throw down the gun and I'll tell you."

"He's telling the truth," Heidi said. "You owe yourself an explanation."

Jira held the pistol in the air like he was in some sort of video game and mulled this, before anger filled his face like an ancient death mask. "I'll be damned if I'm going to listen to a slut, a drunk, or a fag. My God is righteous and will reward me in the next life."

"Do you know what Luis' final words were before he died?" Russell asked.

Jira's face became human again, for the first time in days the tiredness drained, and he was not set upon chaos and destruction. "What did he say?"

"Please tell my father I love him."

Jira closed his eyes and each of them lurched into motion and raced off in different directions. Heidi began sprinting toward the water and the moored powerboat. Russell bent down, picked up the rifle, and lumbered toward the cavern entrance, holding his side. Marley rushed toward the palm trees, his cricket bat in one hand, the military glow stick in the other, like two batons in a relay race. He heard a pained cry from above and a bullet ricocheted off the tree in front of him.

Don't let him target you. This voice inside him sounded fierce, surprisingly like Rex. Who was Marley to argue? He pivoted to his right and found cover behind a second tree, a smaller palm, not quite able to cover his whole torso, even standing sideways. Above, Jira scuttled over to the edge of the ledge closest to Marley and carefully took aim. How many more bullets did this old goat have? Marley surveyed Heidi splashing into the ocean behind him and Russell, pale and quivering, positioning himself at the cavern's edge, trying to find an angle to shoot.

"So, what are your final words, kid?" Jira asked.

"I'm not afraid to be loved by someone," Marley said. "Everyone should have a moment where they see love in the eyes of someone close to them. Like your son must have felt."

This seemed to short-circuit Jira as he tried to process his own emotions in a world where nothing could be controlled. Marley stole a glance to see Heidi treading water next to the boat and Russell circling around the rocks to Jira's backside to try to get an angle. He would need a miracle, another miracle to get out of this one.

Jira smiled and pointed the barrel of the pistol under his chin. His hand quaked and he looked toward the sky. Smoke from the jungle fire floated overhead, blocking the sun. "I can't meet God if I do it myself."

"Let me help you then," Lilian said, racing up behind Jira and shoving him with two hands. The island's self-anointed priest swooped down like an angel, arms outstretched. Almost anything could happen in this dream state, and almost everything did.

The crack of body and wood in the tree boughs dislodged palm fronds and these green tendrils helicoptered to the ground. Marley lost himself in dodging this strange rain of tree limbs and found himself falling back in a dune, spotted with Russell's blood.

"Holy hell," Russell said.

Jira had been impaled in his chest from one of the limbs and hung above the beach, an effigy that reminded Marley of Enrique. Lilian approved of her work and hissed, "An eye for an eye. Old school vengeance."

And just like that Lilian was gone, and Marley wondered if she was now the caye's avenging angel. This island had survived so many invasions over the years and he had no doubt it would be cursed with more. He was done. He wanted to go home, wherever that was, whatever that meant, whoever he now was.

Emotionally spent, Marley barely tracked how Heidi came back to shore and used a shirt from her backpack as a makeshift bandage for Russell, how she held water to his lips that he sipped from muscle memory, the arms on either side of him leading him out and onto the boat. The anchor came up and they all lay back licking their wounds, contemplating their luck and the incomprehensible devastation.

Soaking wet and too exhausted for words, they could see smoke rising above Devil's Caye. For a long stretch none of them spoke, grateful to be alive, breathing deeply in rhythm with the waves lapping the hull, the nightmares of the caye receding as they drifted away.

Marley closed his eyes and was transported to a hotel room overlooking the Eiffel Tower. The carpeting was littered with coconuts and bones, enough to set up a bowling alley for the damned. He lay back on a bed next to his mother covered in a white sheet. She looked out on the cityscape with him, the spires a signal to some faraway entity.

"About time you came to visit me," his mother said.

He fretted about what was under the sheet, what grievous injury she might have sustained.

"I was once a part of you," Marley said.

"That was a different life. A different body. Right now, those buildings cover my arms like hairs. Should I shave them off? Should I start over again?"

"You aren't the earth," Marley said.

"We are all the earth. From the earth. To the earth. Gravity holds us. The tides bind us. The stars warm us. We have forgotten so much."

"Has this happened before? This near extinction?" Marley asked.

"Oh yes, many times and in many different ways."

"Is this even real?" Marley asked.

"If you're brave enough to face it," Heidi answered. "Open your eyes."

The island was barely visible in the darkness. To the east, the sun was rising over the water. So beautiful and serene. Beside them, Russell snored loudly in the boat or else Marley would have wondered if he was dead.

"I had the weirdest dream," Marley said.

"Our bodies adjusted to the new orbit. We slept for an eternity. And my trashcan is empty."

This sounded like something a computer would say. But that made sense, in a way. Their lack of REM had filled up their system with phantoms of their own making, copies of files, a virus now flushed from their system. Yet, the memories remained, and the hallucinations made him question everything he thought he knew. Perhaps this was a good thing.

"Are we dead?" Marley asked.

As though in response, a figure floated toward them on the water at an unnatural speed. It was a woman floating face up in a white dress being pushed by creatures from the sea. Mermaids? Sirens? Then the figure became clearer in the morning glow. It was Kara, in her wedding dress, staring skyward with a dolphin bobbing under each arm, her own ferry service to the next life.

"She is such a lovely bride," Heidi said. "Thanks, girls,"

It took a moment for Marley to realize that she was talking to the dolphins who'd abandoned their task and whisked in close to the boat for Heidi to pet their heads. Their chirps gave him shivers. Marley sneezed and the world shimmered out of focus then back in. Kara was gone.

"We need to get Russell to a hospital," Marley said.

"There's one north of Belize City. By the airport in Vista del Mar. That's where Rick went. That's where we start putting the pieces back together," Heidi said.

Marley started the motor and the dolphins who'd been splashing playfully round the boat moved to give it room to maneuver. The mainland beckoned. So did civilization. Or perhaps not.

Marley would look after his new clan, the three of them survivors of their own worst selves. The actor in him was the poet in him was the son and grandson in him, the many voices of the living and the dead. He opened up the throttle and felt the wind tickling his face. He was waking up. Finally.

"We can leave the worst of ourselves on this island, Marley. We already faced the devil," Heidi said.

Yes, Devil's Caye would soon disappear from sight, but its memories would persist. They had scars. The moon had scars. The world had scars. It felt good to be behind the wheel, to face the world head on. He was awake. They were all, finally, awake. Except Russell, who was still snoring.

Marley steered the boat carefully to avoid hitting the dolphins, now rounding the southwest tip of the island.

"Which way?" he asked.

"Follow them," Heidi said.

CASTLE BRIDGE MEDIA RECOMMENDS...

If you liked *Dream State*, you might also enjoy reading the following titles from Castle Bridge Media available on Amazon or by order at your favorite book store:

Austinites
By In Churl Yo

Bloodsucker City
By Jim Towns

THE CASTLE OF HORROR
ANTHOLOGY SERIES
Volume 1
Volume 2: *Holiday Horrors*
Volume 3: *Scary Summer Stories*
Volume 4: *Women Running From Houses*
Volume 5: *Thinly Veiled: The 70s*
Volume 6: *Femme Fatales**
Volume 7: *Love Gone Wrong*
Volume 8: *Thinly Veiled: The 80s*
Edited By Jason Henderson and
 In Churl Yo
*Edited By P.J. Hoover

Castle of Horror Podcast
Book of Great Horror:
Our Favorites, Top Tens
and Bizarre Pleasures
Edited By Jason Henderson

Dream State
By Martin Ott

FuturePast Sci-Fi Anthology
Edited by In Churl Yo

Isonation
By In Churl Yo

MID-LIFE CRISIS THRILLERS
18 Miles From Town
By Jason Henderson

THE PATH
The Blue-Spangled Blue
By David Bowles
The Deepest Green
By David Bowles

SURF MYSTIC
Night of the Book Man
By Peyton Douglas

Nightwalkers: Gothic Horror Movies
By Bruce Lanier Wright

Yesterday's Tomorrows:
The Golden Age of Science Fiction
Movie Posters
By Bruce Lanier Wright

Please remember to leave us your reviews on Amazon and Goodreads!

THANK YOU FOR SUPPORTING INDEPENDENT PUBLISHERS AND AUTHORS!
castlebridgemedia.com